BEASTS' LEGACY

Past, Present & Future

Rey Maya

Casa Rei

First Casa Rei English edition: August 2025
Originally published in Spanish as El Legado de los Monstruos in July 2025.

ISBN-13: 979-8-9993737-4-8 (Paperback - Cream paper)
ISBN-13: 979-8-9993737-5-5 (Hardcover - White paper)
ISBN-13: 979-8-9993737-6-2 (Hardcover – Cream paper)

CONTENTS

PREFACE

I wrote these stories because I am not afraid. These are not classic horror tales, nor are they contrived fiction about mythical beings that roar in the darkness. There are no dragons here, no ogres, no vampires. You will not find zombies. There are no ghosts.

The beasts in my book are of a different kind—closer, more terrible. They are the ones who speak calmly, who smile across the dinner table, who justify themselves in the name of duty or of love. They are the monsters that weave their webs with the threads of a fine and impeccable logic, and who devour with reason.

I have learned to see them through their effects. They are everywhere, though they camouflage themselves in the mundane, behind custom, normality, and progress. They hide among us because, as fierce as they may seem, they are deeply terrified of goodness and truth. They tremble before the courage a single human being can have to confront them. They fear the pen that names them, the eye that recognizes them, the voice that refuses to be silent.

This work is an attempt to amputate their claws, a kind of bestiary of the monsters that walk beside us, or on our own feet, and that leave behind the deepest, most painful tracks.

I have hunted them in the past, brought them down from their thrones. I have trapped them in the present, in the coldness of systems, pulled them from homes, and even from the trash. I have tried to glimpse their shadows in the future that awaits us, where, without a doubt, they will also dwell.

But I know they are not all here; they could not be. There are many other beasts I could not contain in these pages. Some, because they are too perceptive, too skilled at slipping through the cracks of a verse. Others, because they don't go out much. They remain hidden, crouching in a complicit silence, in the corners I have not yet been able to illuminate, until the time comes.

My next hunt.

Because the beasts, the real ones, are always there. They are the same as they have always been. And this is only a part of their story. A sparse account of their devastation.

That is why I now invite you. I invite you to stay, to let yourself be surprised and ensnared by these tales that may make you laugh, but also cry. I invite you to use these pages as a resource to find the tools to make your own beasts pay.

And above all, I invite you to shout. Not in terror at the evil revealed here, but with the firm voice of one who refuses to remain silent. To shout to expose them, to name them, to annihilate them... before they, with their calm and their impeccable reasons, do it to you.

Consider this book one more small tool for that path you may have, without knowing it, already begun to walk.

To you, who dare to taste a coffee from a distant harvest:

May its flavor inspire you to seek the root of

your own peace. And to care for it.

—RM.

PAST

Echoes of Forgotten Kingdoms

THE EDGE OF TRUTH

Some write to rule.
Others rule so nothing gets written.
But there are quills that serve neither.

The King ruled without opposition or criticism from atop a golden throne, surrounded by high walls and low words. No one defied him. No one questioned him. No one described him without permission. It was said his rule brought order, but that order was built on fear, obedience, and hunger.

The markets were empty, and stomachs even more so. And yet, within the palace walls hung portraits showing plentiful smiles and bread on every table. Portraits drawn by words, and those words written by only one man: the royal scribe.

That man, for years, had turned the people's silence into the King's speeches. But one day, he died.

The King, more unsettled by the vacancy than saddened by the loss, summoned all the scribes in the realm. He needed to appoint a new voice—his shield of ink. The requirement was simple: each candidate had to write a text, a facsimile of his reign. All of them had to use the same pen—the late scribe's.

The butler presented the King with a narrow box made of dark wood. Inside rested the pen. It was a dull black, slightly tinged with blue, like the wings of certain crows in sunlight. Long and curved, with a firm, sharp quill tip capped by a faintly gleaming metallic point—as if it had once been gold. Its very presence commanded a strange respect. It weighed no more than air, yet when held, it felt as though it carried the memory of all it had ever written. The butler presented it with a terse instruction: "It's what he requested."

The monarch didn't question the dying man's final wish, for he had been a wise servant who had helped preserve his power through eloquent, irrefutable speeches. In the end, the verdict would be his alone.

For days, submissions poured in—many nearly identical, full of repeated formulas and empty phrases. But two texts stood out

—not for their beauty, but for how starkly they opposed each other. Intrigued and pleased, the King ordered both to be read before the full court.

First, the more ornamental one:

"In this Kingdom, no one knows want, under the tireless gaze of His Majesty. Discipline and order are the foundation of our prosperity. Citizens walk safely, without fear or doubt, because thought is unified, clear and firm. All we have we owe to the strong hand that guides us. There are no divisive voices, no misleading gestures: only unity. Long live stability! Long live the will of the King!"

Applause erupted—a shower of ovations. The King nodded, satisfied. Then the second was read:

"In this Kingdom, hunger isn't only served on the plate—it's in the voice that cannot rise. Bread is scarce... but scarcer still is the right to say it is. Order is demanded, but fear is what reigns. People do not speak aloud. Nor do they dream. They only repeat. Only survive. The King wants servants, not citizens. And so, no one dares write what they feel. Until today."

The room froze—not in respect, but in vertigo. Then the butler stepped forward and held out a sealed scroll. "Your Majesty," he said, "the scribe asked me to give you this at this precise moment."

The King, still puzzled, broke the seal and read aloud:

"This pen does not serve the King. It serves the truth. Whoever takes it will not write what they want... but what they carry inside. At times, it will echo the voice of power. At others, what power fears most. But it will never lie. Because to write with this pen is to write unmasked."

The King descended from his platform and walked to the center of the hall, where the pen rested on a pedestal. He looked at the two finalists—one held his gaze, the other did not know where to look. Then he spoke: "Both wrote with it. And both revealed the truth. The truth of the one who whispers in fear to serve, and the truth that a man shouts when he can no longer remain silent."

He picked up the pen slowly. "From today on, this Kingdom shall have two scribes. One to tell the King's story... and one to tell it to him alone."

Since then, every decree was written with two voices: the voice of power, and that of the soul that still dared to write with trembling hands. For a tyrant may rule in silence, but he will never survive the truth.

Power fears the edge of truth. But even more, it fears the weight of a pen that writes without permission.

MADE TO MEASURE
FOR THE KING

He who obeys makes no mistake—
in the eyes of mistaken power.

There, where everything was stitched with the thread of tradition and royal will, the King ordered a new ceremonial suit. Not out of vanity... or perhaps it was. He wanted to wear it for the solemn nuptials of the prince and his bride-to-be. He had to look impeccable. Radiant. Befitting a King. The royal tailor, with weathered hands and long silences, took his measurements with care, selected the finest fabrics from the ancestral wardrobe, and spent days crafting a garment fit for the crown.

On the eve of the event, the King donned his new attire in front of the tall mirrors of the Octagonal Hall. That's when he noticed it: the right sleeve hung lower than the left. Only by a few fingers, but enough to sound an alarm. "Is one of my arms longer than the other?" he wondered, fishing for some trace of betrayal in the depths of his mind. He immediately summoned the Royal Physician.

The doctor arrived with his leather case, his cautious gait, and his slick, patent-leather voice trained never to contradict. The King extended his arms firmly and said, "Look. Look closely." The physician examined him with all the gravity the situation required. He held both arms, compared them, tapped here and there, and ran his wise fingers over them. After a silence longer than a sealed report, he glanced at the tailor for a moment, then turned back to the monarch and said, "Your Majesty... your arms are perfectly equal."

"And what about the uneven sleeves?" the King asked.

The physician sighed. "With your permission, Sire... you don't need a doctor. You need a new tailor."

The King slowly lowered his arms. The only sound was the ticking of the pendulum clock, like a hangman's drumroll. The tailor lowered his gaze. "The cut is exact, Your Majesty," he replied, trembling, "according to the measurements."

"And what if the measurements were wrong?" said the King. The tailor did not answer. He only bowed his head and swallowed hard.

From that day on, the King didn't have the suit corrected; he corrected his posture. He learned to walk with one arm discreetly bent and ordered his portraits adjusted so the longer side was always hidden beneath the royal mantle. He commissioned new garments, all with the same asymmetry. And soon, the entire court began to imitate him. Because in that Kingdom, no one corrected the King. It was the King who corrected the mirror.

REY MAYA

THE WET NURSE

He who robs the poor of their bread
will one day beg for their mercy.

I n the distant Southern Region, far from the palace, the peasants clawed at the earth with their bare hands. The soil was infertile—rough and dry—despite the river that ran across the kingdom, which in that forgotten land dwindled into thin, dying streams.

There, where justice never seemed to arrive, lived a woman. Poor and alone. Her hut was the only thing left standing after she had lost everything: her son, her cow, her goat, the water in her well, and even her hens, stolen away by the cunning strike of an eagle. The land she owned yielded nothing but weeds.

One day, while gathering firewood near the river, she saw a snake trapped in the eagle's talons—the same bird she had once cursed with fury. She recognized it well: one wing was wounded, marked by a rebellious white feather that stood out from the rest and made its flight lopsided, like a persistent curse. She couldn't miss the chance to strike back. She hurled her stick with the precision of an archer, striking the predator and, unintentionally, freeing the snake, which slithered away into the leaves.

When she returned home, there it was... the cow. In the yard. Tied to the almond tree that barely cast a shadow anymore. Just as before, as if time had rewound. This time it looked healthier, its udders brimming. Its milk was dense, white as snow, with a flavor even honey couldn't rival. That cow brought her comfort and companionship. She sold and bartered the milk, and with the rest, she made cheese that fed half the village. People called it magic—and maybe it was. Though the land grew only thorns, the cow always looked well-fed, and its milk was sweet and abundant.

The Queen gave birth to a son, but her body produced no milk. Wet nurses dried up, like everything else that had once been fertile. Word of the cow reached the castle. Rumor had it the milk cured insomnia, restored appetite, and strengthened bones. The King—a man possessed by, and possessor of, every kind of wealth—couldn't let the opportunity pass. "Bring me the animal," he commanded. And the cow was confiscated. But the milk soured, the cow dried up, and it died.

Time passed, and yet there was still cheese on the woman's table. One morning, right where the cow had stood, the goat appeared—thin, but with the same silver-eyed gaze.

Once again, she had milk. Once again, the villagers came to her door. The Kingdom, now watching the village closely, heard the news and sent for the goat. And just like before... it dried up.

Then, one dawn, the woman heard a murmur coming from the old well. She approached the stone rim and saw white foam. She drew up a bucket. It was milk. "The breast of the earth nourishes us!" the people cried, and their voices echoed all the way to the throne. The King issued a decree: he declared the entire area property of the Crown and expelled the woman. Stripped of everything, she began to beg, supported only by the charity of those who still remembered her gift. It didn't take long for the well itself to run dry and offer only dust.

It seemed the land itself had been cursed. The rivers dried, the soil cracked, breasts were flaccid and empty. Death galloped unbridled through the streets and palace corridors. They said the Queen had been bitten by a snake that slithered into her sheets and died before dawn. The little Prince was left motherless and milkless. One by one, the wet nurses failed. Throughout the Kingdom, mothers stopped lactating, and babies sickened and died.

That night, the King couldn't sleep. When exhaustion finally overtook him, he dreamed of his wife—but it wasn't the Queen he had loved. It was a shadowy figure, transformed. Her face was distorted, and from the base of her torso emerged a scaled tail that rose like a menacing whip. He could only stare, hypnotized by her cruel eyes, as the specter approached. Then he heard the hiss of her forked tongue, tracing a sentence in the air: "Find the woman. The milk from her cow, her goat, and her well is no sweeter than that from her own breast."

The King awoke in a cold sweat, chilled to the bone. And he understood—abundance could be seized, but only by those who first deserved it. He summoned her—not to confiscate, but as a silent and solemn invitation to the bread he had once taken, to the roof he had torn away. He offered her lodging in the palace, a new shelter, and a new title: guardian.

Even then, he remained enchanted—driven either by the urge to preserve his kingdom or by that haunting revelation. He offered her the challenge and the burden of nursing the Prince, who had turned yellow with illness, and of sustaining his life with her own.

She accepted. She had nothing left to lose. Her breasts had swelled the moment she crossed the palace threshold. As soon as the child touched her skin, life surged forth—milk gushed from her body. The boy latched on with strength and closed his eyes in peace.

A year passed. The child grew strong, though he never lost the peculiar color in his skin and eyes. And when he finally learned to say "mother," his amber eyes didn't seek the crown. They sought her.

Mothers regained their milk. The rivers returned to their banks. The land turned green again. And the woman became a mother once more—to a child, and to a Kingdom.

BLACK CARDAMOM

The one who bows his head...
God shall crown.

The night before the Day of Grace, the palace kitchen smelled of glory and grief. The recent sorrow over the King's death did not dampen the feast, but it did cast a shadow on every face. The head cook—a man of ancient habits and liturgical hands—moved among pots and braziers with the skill of an alchemist. He gave orders with a firm voice, tasted every dish with almost priestly precision, and had the custom of saying a short prayer in Latin before plating.

The Scepter Supper was a traditional rite, attended by nobles from the four corners of the realm. That night, they served wine-braised lamb, pears stewed with honey and cloves, rosemary-braided bread, almond cream, and a selection of aged cheeses. The finishing touch was a warm infusion of imperial spices—among them, black cardamom.

Few knew the true origins of that meticulous cook. The tale went that one foggy morning, the monks of the Domus Dei Monastery spotted a well bucket floating downstream with a child inside—a new Moses. They raised him as one of their own, teaching him Latin, rhetoric, writing, and the culinary arts, with all their secret recipes. He was good at everything, yet none of it was his true calling. Before receiving the tonsure, the Abbot called him into private audience and released him from his vow with a blessing. Recognizing his gift in the kitchen, the Abbot procured for him a letter of recommendation to the royal household. And so, he entered through the kitchen door, head held high, ladle ready.

Morning broke, and heralds galloped down the roads proclaiming, "Coronation at Terce!" The blind Archbishop waited in the cathedral's presbytery, his worn ivory mitre and hands firm upon the golden crown. Hymns floated among the frescoes and pillars, while incense rose like a prayer given form. Nobles took their seats with poise and elegance, and the commoners, packed tightly and full of anticipation, waited for the procession.

"Let the one to be crowned approach," the clergyman announced.

And the yellow-hued Prince advanced with solemn cadence.

At that very hour, the cook was overwhelmed with preparations for the celebration feast. As he reached for the spices, he saw something that froze his blood: a snake clinging to the jar of black cardamom. He remembered the Queen—dead from a serpent's bite—and the phrase carved into the monastery's refectory beam: Ubi serpens cenat, vita periclitatur ("Where the serpent dines, life is in peril"). He crossed himself and ran.

No one expected him to burst into the sacred hall—sweaty, covered in flour and grease. The monks feared the worst. The Abbot opened his mouth but said nothing. The nobles recoiled, and the yellow Prince froze mid-step, seeming to lose what little color he had. The cook, breathless and frantic, slipped on the polished floor and fell to his knees—head bowed as if begging forgiveness.

The blind Archbishop heard the footsteps and sensed the presence. He lowered the crown and placed it on the cook's head. In that instant, the stained glass exploded with light and a thunderclap without sound split the air. The one they had taken for a Prince let out a shriek.

Everyone opened their eyes—and saw only a King.

The cook closed his own and accepted the weight of the crown. The Archbishop never saw... he merely crowned the one who was meant to be crowned.

CROSS AND PYRE

A fire that spares none, cares for none.

How does one recognize a witch? The Kingdom was full of them.

Women who gathered alone to talk. Women who bore no children. Women who looked men straight in the eye, who prepared ointments with herbs and walked alone at night. Women who dared to speak of their dreams, who could read and write, and who helped others give birth without the Church's blessing.

The Kingdom was infested with them, and since they couldn't burn their freedom, they burned their bodies.

Once a month, the pyre was lit in the main square. Smoke rose, chants echoed, and the people—afraid of seeming complicit—applauded every sentence. The Archbishop, as tall and gaunt as the staff he clung to, had hawk's eyes and a judge's gaze. He claimed to read the soul by the shape of the face, and no one dared to contradict him.

But not all fires burned in the square; some burned in silent alleys, in locked homes, or in whispers that reached the very tapestries of the castle. That month, a disturbing rumor began to circulate—one that grazed the throne: the birth of an illegitimate child, the result of an affair between the crown prince and a peasant woman from the South.

The Archbishop, who deep down knew that blood is harder to hide than sin, made no delay and handled the matter "with discretion." Hooded men fell upon the woman and took her child. They didn't kill him, but they made her believe they had—leaving a cloth soaked in hen's blood under the dry almond tree in her yard. It was enough to shatter the poor peasant woman's soul, leaving her the mother of a dead child she could never bury.

The child was given to the Archbishop, who personally arranged for him to be taken to the Domus Dei monastery. "He is to be raised in silence," he ordered. "He is to learn, and he is not to be known."

And so he locked away his transgression in a cell without bars: the cell of forgetting.

Years passed. The prince rose to the throne upon his father's death, and with him, his wife—a woman of gentle speech, graceful movements, and ashen eyes. Perhaps a princess, perhaps not.

Her charm dazzled all who beheld her, even the old Archbishop, in whose hands he steadily placed the Kingdom's destiny.

The burnings did not stop. The purifying fervor multiplied. Women were condemned for walking barefoot, for letting their hair loose, for giving birth without pain, for menstruating under a full moon, or simply for refusing to lower their gaze.

That year, a midwife was brought to trial. She knew of herbs and births, and had saved many poor women—but power does not forgive those who earn respect without divine permission. The young woman was declared a witch and sentenced to burn like the others.

The square was packed. Monks chanted their litanies and soldiers fed the fire. The clergyman, wearing mitre and staff, stood at the foot of the pyre, as was his holy office. It was his duty to hold the cross high, in sight of the condemned, so she might still save her soul.

He was accustomed to hiding the blood on his hands beneath spotless silk gloves, over which his episcopal ring gleamed.

But the young woman neither lowered her gaze, nor raised her voice. The flames rose, and the scent of burning flesh tore through the air. Amid the smoke, a single spark—just one—rose like a firefly and spiraled up until it touched the old man's face.

It wasn't large. It didn't burn him. But it blinded him forever.

THE WITCH AND
THE GODDESS

The good man wins when he learns to defend himself—
when he defends his cause tooth and nail.

He hadn't gone south in search of treasure, but for something simpler: adventure, wind on his face, and maybe a little dirt under his nails. He fled the palace, his golden cage, and rode with the curiosity of someone who had never seen the world beyond the walls.

She was gathering firewood by the river, the same routine at the same border. Poor, young, with thick braids and a clear, glimmering gaze. She tripped and twisted her ankle. And he—still a man without a story—lifted her onto his horse, relieving her of the weight of her firewood, her path, and her solitude. They kept meeting, at first with excuses, and later with none. Then desire grew: youthful, awkward, innocent. A desire that can't be measured, calculated, or contained. He didn't know he would love her. She didn't know she would birth a king.

His Majesty found out, and the weight of the scepter fell on his son like an anvil. The scandal could cost him the throne, so he punished him, locked him away, and threatened to disinherit him. He forced him to marry a daughter of nobody, born into some forgotten house extinguished by old wars. But she had something men often mistook for nobility: beauty, a silky voice, and ashen eyes that seemed to see from a place older than time. The Princess wasn't chosen—she was imposed with a seductive and insinuating softness.

By the time the Prince accepted the marriage, he was no longer quite himself—nor was his father. They both slept more and questioned less, and what once were their own thoughts now echoed a female voice heard in their dreams. The Prince succeeded his father, and as was custom, the hand of God legitimized his throne through the Archbishop.

The new Queen had brought peace—at least, to her dark desire: throne, power, and luxury. But that which we resist persists, and the forgotten woman of the South reappeared.

"A son of the King, alive, in the South," whispered the wind, bursting from fountains and slipping through palace walls.

And then came the fury. The desire to erase anything not her own.

She summoned men who were neither soldiers nor noblemen—they were those with no names and no inheritance. The order was clear: find the woman and take the child. But, as always, the story took a turn. In the tavern, as they drank and toasted to the new Queen, one of the thugs was overheard saying, "An easy job, this time." Another asked, "What if someone finds out?" The first one replied, "Who's going to talk? The kid doesn't even have teeth."

A shadow rose from the corner, left a few coins on the bar, and disappeared without a sound.

That night, she held her child close, unaware it could be the last time. The men's steps were already near—some sent by the Queen, others in the name of the Archbishop, who had been warned.

The clergy's messengers reached her first. They asked for the child, saying his life depended on it. Desperate, she clung to the baby, but when she heard the shouting, the wood splintering, and the vile voices, she wrapped him in his blanket, kissed him without goodbye, and let him go.

The Queen's men found nothing but a wounded, empty mother. Furious, they searched for clues, but the well-meaning abductors faked the boy's death, leaving behind the birthing cloth stained with hen's blood in their frantic escape. They were never seen again.

The bloodied proof was delivered to the Queen, and the child was given to the Archbishop. The bandits returned to the South under royal orders and laid the cloth beneath the old almond tree.

Both women had been deceived—by two kinds of thieves, equally cowardly. One could not bury her child; the other could not bury her ambition.

"If a son could dethrone me," thought the Queen, "then let us make a son."

In the solitude of her chamber, the Queen shaped her thoughts. She stole the massive, consecrated paschal candle that burned day and night in the royal chapel. With her dagger, she cut and sculpted it while whispering words in a tongue no one knew.

When the final feature was complete, she blew on the creation, and it seemed to flicker—alive, like a candle lit for the first time.

It had been born. But everything born must be fed.

She called the wet nurses. All failed. The creature cried without a voice and cracked from within.

So, the Queen reached for her dagger, cut her palm, and let a few drops of blood fall.

The blood touched the burnished blade, and on its surface appeared a vision: a cow in a faraway southern land, with overflowing udders and milk that was white, thick, and sweet. She convinced the King to seize it, speaking of health, of wealth in milk, of royal duty. The King, entranced, agreed.

But it didn't work.

The cow dried up, and the child grew cold. The spell wavered. The Queen herself slaughtered the cow, letting its blood soak the dagger.

A new image appeared: a thin goat with silver eyes. The goat was brought—but it, too, was emptied and rendered useless.

The cycle repeated: she spilled that blood and consulted the blade.

This time, the image was of an old cracked well, overflowing with white milk rising from the rim like manna.

The well was seized, along with the land and that miserable house. The peasant woman was left to wander, having lost everything. The well dried up soon after.

Desperate, the Queen placed the dagger on the table. She had no more victims, nothing left to sacrifice. The blade was mute— no vision, no reflection, no milk.

Only one blood remained: that of the woman she had already stripped of everything.

Her eyes sharpened. Her dagger was ready.

That's when the serpent appeared.

It slid across the stone with the grace of a shadow and the certainty of something already written.

It was no ordinary serpent—its body was slender, but its presence filled the room.

Its gaze was deep, beyond time, as if it remembered the moment the world was created.

The Queen sprang to her feet and raised the dagger, trying to utter an incantation—one of those she had whispered so many times into the King's sleeping ear.

But the words failed.

The serpent did not stop. It struck.

The Queen screamed and fought, but no spell, no dagger, could shield her from the judgment of a goddess.

Her body convulsed, her eyes lost their light, and she collapsed backward without a sound.

The dagger slipped from her fingers, and the serpent, after one final glance, disappeared into shadow.

And the Queen—the crowned witch—lay alone, her power extinguished, her mask shattered, while not far away, her abomination cried.

WITHIN WALLS

We all want to go back home.

The Kingdom lived within walls. Tall, solid, ancient. Not quite as high as mountains—but just as high as the life expectancy of those who had never seen what lay beyond them. Within those borders, life was peaceful and harmonious—or so everyone said.

The desire to know what was outside was nearly nonexistent, because people believed they were happy, and that was enough.

Until one day, a giant bird crossed the sky, carrying a child from the province away in its belly.

For the first time, doubt stirred.

Theories were born, grew, matured into uneasy curiosity —and the Kingdom's tranquility aged and died. The scholars warned of beasts beyond the borders. The bards turned it into myth: giants with feet of iron and bottomless hunger; fiends with bloodthirsty fangs and piercing cries.

Panic spread.

The people doubled down.

They turned their walls into sacred relics, decorated them with murals and slogans. The more they fortified the Kingdom, the weaker words became. The more they smothered thought, the hotter faith burned.

Years passed.

One night, while the town slept the sweet sleep of the undisturbed, a giant bird descended into the plaza and spat out the child who had once been stolen by the skies.

He was now a man.

By sunrise, word of his return spread through the Kingdom like wildfire. The King summoned him, gathered the court, and brought him before the people.

The man spoke—calmly, but with fire in his voice. He told of his long years beyond the walls. Of breathtaking landscapes, smoking mountains, deserts and forests. Of dreamlike places where houses were taller than the Kingdom's walls, lit by eternal sources of light. Of riders soaring through the skies atop great birds. Of magic boxes filled with tiny living people—a puppet show come to life, telling marvelous tales. Of books without pages, where moving images danced like soothsayers in crystal balls. Of messages that crossed oceans in the blink of an eye.

When he finished, the people burst into laughter.

They mocked his tale—and him.

The King, stern-faced, declared him mad. He claimed the man was cursed, infected with the madness of the outer world. And, for the sake of order and peace, sentenced him to live out his days in the castle dungeons.

A fitting punishment for someone who dared to disturb the harmony of a Kingdom.

Years later, on his deathbed, the King called for the prisoner once more and received him in private.

"I must confess something," the monarch said. "I believe every word you spoke. I know what you saw. I too once lived beyond these walls."

The man stared at him—stunned, bewildered.

"Then why, Your Majesty," he asked, "did you order my imprisonment?"

The King closed his eyes for a moment, then whispered:

"Because in a Kingdom built within walls... madmen could never be allowed to rule. And here, there can only be one King."

Then, the King closed his eyes for good.

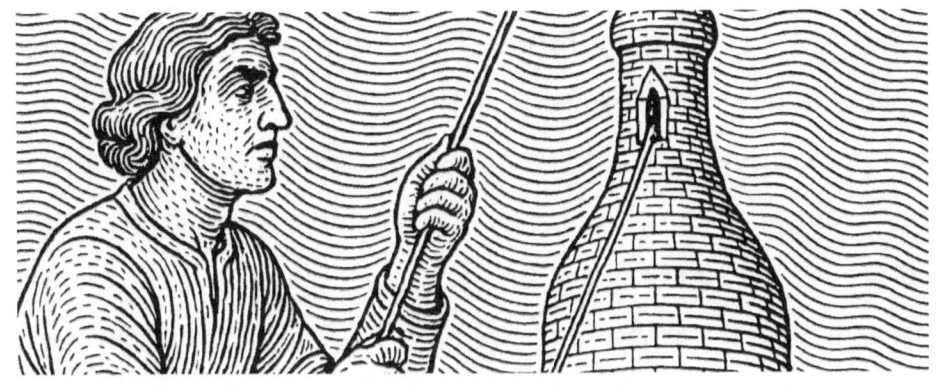

A-LIVE

Being together is not the same as knowing each other.

When the King's breath faded like shadows at dusk, a tower rose in the heart of the Kingdom —the cruelest of all—popularly known as "The Bottle." It wasn't a watchtower or fortress, but a tube to bottle a body, a prison to crush the spirit. A single barred window crowned the structure like a mocking eye, blind to the darkness below where the prisoner withered. At the bottom of this stone bottle suffered Jonah. To the King's court, he was a madman condemned for his Tales from Beyond the Walls. But to the people who whispered in markets and taverns, such a harsh punishment for a mere "madman" seemed madness in itself

—either Jonah's, or the King's. That's why some curious souls would linger near the base of the tower, hoping to stumble upon a trace of bottled truth. Rashad, more curious than the rest, sought contact. For weeks, he tried throwing stones, then improved his aim with a sling. Finally, after countless attempts, he achieved it: a thin rope, carefully weighted, slipped through the barred eye of The Bottle and descended into the void.

To Jonah, who had seen nothing but stone and a distant sliver of sky for years, the rope sliding before him was an apparition. Too fragile to climb and too narrow an opening to escape, the rope was more than a thread—it was a chance to see blindly. He pulled twice. Tug-Tug. No code. No plan. Just a receipt of contact to the sky, to the stranger. A way to say, "I'm here."

Outside, Rashad felt the vibration in his sweaty hands. His heart leapt. He's alive! The madman is alive! Holding his breath, he respectfully returned the cadence. Tug-Tug.

Inside, Jonah felt the answering pull, and in that instant, the dungeon, the King, and the years of solitude vanished. He had connection. Knowing that there was a thinking mind at the other end, a soul responding, gave him breath he thought long lost. His two pulls were met with the same response. A language. A conversation. Life itself speaking. No words, yet everything was said. In that first exchange, they had built a language and spoken the first word of their new world—the only one that mattered. Two tugs: A-LIVE.

The rope visits continued. Days became months, and months became the King's final year. The Bottle felt unbearably hollow when the rope didn't dance, that thread that carried warm, fresh communication inside. The language evolved. From the primal affirmation A-LIVE, they developed a rustic Morse code, where the number of tugs conveyed a full idea. Or so they believed.

In the last hour of the King's last day, The Bottle shattered —along with the walls—brought down by an enraged people's hunger for freedom. Jonah was summoned before the dying monarch.

"I too was outside the walls," the King whispered. "Neither of us is mad. You struck me with truth, and I shielded myself with lies. So, I crowned lies and bottled truth." And then he died—his power, laws, the people's fears, and the walls with him.

Oh, what a surprise for Jonah to meet Rashad! Still clinging to that rope of sorrow, weeping at the silence on the other end. Oh, what a shock to meet, embrace, and discover that their dictionary, born from distance and darkness, had two translations.

Now they stood there, minds clouded before the tower. The One Inside and the One Outside.

"Lucas! We did it!" cried the one outside, tears of joy streaming down his face.

Jonah, confused by how he had been called and by the blinding sun, could barely stand.

"I had faith," he said. "Each day I sent you my prayers and invited you to join me: LET'S-PRAY."

Outside, under the sun, Rashad felt those two jolts as a command: FIGHT-NOW. And so he asked: WHAT-TO-DO?

Jonah had understood: YES-I-DO. And he told himself, "What zeal this man has!"

Silence fell, deeper than the dungeon.

"I thanked you," whispered Jonah—THANK-YOU-KIND-LY.

"And I heard it as," said Rashad — RISE-IN-THE-STREETS.

Jonah looked into his eyes, finally understanding what had sparked the revolution. "I said: I'M-PRAY-ING-FOR-YOU."

Rashad covered his face, and a laugh—strange and tearful—broke from his chest. "And I heard: TEAR-THE-WALLS-ALL-DOWN. And I did! I rallied the people, inspired by your example. We rose up and brought down the walls."

The man who had only offered prayers looked at the freed Kingdom—freed by a mistranslation. Two perspectives, two channels, hanging by a fragile thread. One signal, two meanings.

He placed a hand on his liberator's shoulder. "What a testimony of courage and strategy, Caleb. My faith and prayers were with you. By the way, my name is JO-NAH, not Lucas."

Out of habit, he tapped twice on the shoulder, the first tap firmer.

Rashad wiped his tears, still laughing. "Nice to meet you, Jonah. I'm RA-SHAD, not Caleb."

He returned the gesture—two pats on the back, the second one longer—sealing at last, face to face, the one and only message they had always understood:

A-LIVE.

PRESENT

Echoes of Inner Noise

THE WORLD IS INSANE

Madness doesn't always beg.

Once upon a time, there was a woman everyone called crazy. She lived under a bridge, in the middle of a colossal city.

Every morning, she went out early, wandering the streets aimlessly. She rummaged through trash as if searching for treasures—and sometimes she found them: a broken brooch, a single, partnerless shoe, a bottle.

She wore bulky headphones, the kind that cover your entire ears, fitted to her head as if she'd been born with them. She wore them like a part of her body and never took them off.

She walked with her head down, muttering, maybe humming melodies no one could hear. She only looked up to protest to the sky—about the rain, the heat, or the mere fact that the sky was still there. At night, she returned under the bridge, where her only company was rats and her thoughts.

One day, another madman came along. He was thin, with the look of someone who had read too much and eaten too little. He wore a buttoned-up shirt, tattered pants held up with shoelaces, and always carried a comb hanging from his waist like a talisman. His glasses were thick and crooked, one arm held together by a strip of cloth, and he clutched a book to his chest as if his entire soul were inside it. He wandered the city handing out ideas and collecting scraps—like a ragged philosopher no one paid attention to.

"What are you listening to?" he asked the woman.

She looked at him with a smile and replied, "Nothing!"

"Nothing?" he repeated, baffled. "Then why wear headphones?" The woman furrowed her brow, as if she didn't understand. Then she said:

"Don't you know? The world is insane.

I don't wear headphones to hear—I wear them not to listen. Because the mad... shouldn't be listened to."

DREAM AND NIGHTMARE

Some have died for a dream.
And some live without ever waking.
The latter are more dead.

O n the other side of the sea, in a land without a name or a future, an old dreamer watched his dreams come true. Everything he dreamed became reality. Whether it was joyful or dreadful, clear or incomprehensible, his world awakened to the shape of his inner night. He was a visionary asleep.

Once, he dreamed of an empire collapsing. The walls fell, statues toppled, plazas emptied, slogans faded, and flags stopped waving.

Another time, he dreamed of a pandemic sweeping the world. He saw masked faces, bodies stacked, the wailing of many and the silence of all. And soon after, he dreamed of the cure, and the outbreak ceased.

Until one night, he had a stormy dream. He dreamed of himself. A second self —identical, but paler, older, more real— approached him in silence, knelt beside his bed, and whispered in his ear: "You will stop dreaming. And someone in your house will die."

The old man thought of his wife and daughter. He trembled for both. And fearing more for them than for the loss of his gift, he refused to awaken.

He fought to remain inside his lucid dream, determined to keep the prophecy from coming true. He filled his realm with imaginary characters, held dialogues, forged stories, and set endless appointments.

He filled an enormous calendar with events only he would remember.

And so, time passed —days, years— submerged in a world growing ever denser, ever deeper.

A world with no threshold and no return.

Another dream fulfilled.

FUNERALS

The dead to the grave, the living to the feast.

I n a small Mexican town, the Comisario died. As the enormous funeral procession made its way toward the village cemetery, a journalist—sent to cover the event— remarked pensively to a lean-faced man who had joined the tail end of the cortege.

"He must have been deeply loved," said the reporter. "I've never seen so many people at a burial."

"Not at all," the man replied without flinching. "He was the most despicable of men—greedy, manipulative, and cruel. During his time in office, the town's savings vanished, the dignity of the poor was trampled, and only those freedoms that bowed to his decrees were allowed."

"Then... why are they here?" the reporter asked. "Wouldn't they have stayed away out of contempt?"

"They're not here because of how they feel," the man said, his eyes fixed on the casket. "You don't pay tribute to a monster who trades freedom for dependence. They're here because they know that once the slab is sealed, the grieving family will serve the best mole in town."

MASS-PRODUCED CHILDREN

Desire preserves, indifference extinguishes.

L ong ago, when children were still well made, child factories were thriving. They were assembled carefully, one by one, atop slow-gestation tables. Their components were simple yet priceless: love, tenderness, dreams, and a bit of clay. At every stage, their humanity was tested, and once completed, they were sent out in their original packaging, with a standard-issue smile, to homes where adults were still willing to raise them. It was a time of expansion, a time of humanity.

But the factories began to shut down — not because the machines failed, but because the orders stopped coming.

Interest waned, and the market turned to more convenient industries. Self-image factories took over the catalogs, specializing in morpho-surgical enhancement, aesthetic grafts, and interchangeable faces. The booming industry of bodily gadgets followed: smart devices, embedded visors, implantable assistants, and emotional control chips. Pet factories also flourished, offering obedient, on-demand affection in customizable models.

Anything that didn't require nurturing, bonding, or unpredictability was favored. Children, on the other hand, came without warranties. They were expensive, they cried, and they took years to function properly. Some arrived with defects; others were canceled before shipping or discarded unopened.

And so, the factories shut down. No hands remained willing to mold a soul, and no machine could imitate one without a clear design. Humanity grew old. Cribs rusted. The world became a waiting room without play.

Then, a group of engineers proposed an alternative model: not to manufacture children, but to rebuild the human being using the materials at hand.

They gave them fire for brains, so they would think fast: no pause, no doubt. Ice for hearts, so they wouldn't feel, empathize, or hesitate. Stones for eyes: hard, dull, incapable of betraying emotion or intent. And instead of feet, they fitted them with air turbines, so they'd be light and unburdened.

Thus, the modern man was born. He's completely burned out. He deals in coldness. He sees no one but himself. And his feet never touch the ground.

The rest are outdated models, devalued and nearly extinct.

MEDICAL RECORD

I'm not what I say.
I'm what you don't see.

The doctor didn't look up when the patient walked in. She typed with an automatic rhythm, like someone repeating a gesture learned more from defense than from duty.

"Good afternoon. Please have a seat. Full name, please."

The woman sat down carefully, tucked her purse between her legs, and replied in a low voice, "I don't know. I don't remember."

The doctor typed: *Patient does not state name. Possible memory impairment.*

"Age?"

"Eighty-something, I think."

"Height?"

"Five-foot-one, maybe less. I've been shrinking lately."

"Weight?"

"Whatever the scale says, doctor. But you haven't weighed me yet."

The doctor smiled, still not looking at her. "Daily routine?"

The patient thought for a moment. "I get up late, because there's no rush. Sometimes I have breakfast, if I remember. I walk around the house, do small chores, and help my daughter in the kitchen when I can."

"Do you live with your daughter?" the doctor asked, without looking up.

"Not exactly. She lives with me, but she leaves early and comes home late. She works a lot. Sometimes I hear her crying in the shower, but then she smiles at me and turns on the TV. She leaves the soap operas playing for me. I like them, though I sometimes get the characters confused."

"Do you know why you're here?"

"For my chest," said the woman, placing a hand over her heart. "It hurts when I'm alone. Here. Like something is tightening inside, but it's not my heart, it's something further back. Like a door that won't shut properly."

"How long has this been going on?"

"I don't know. I forget sometimes. But when I remember, it hurts."

The doctor began typing faster: *Female patient, elderly. Nonspecific chest pain, no radiation. Episodic. Associated with loneliness and periods of rest.*

She added a few more lines, with a learned gesture of fatigue: *Consistent with subclinical anxiety. Possible psychosomatic component.*

She paused briefly.

"I'm going to prescribe something mild. Alpirexan. A gentle relaxant. It won't interfere with your other medications. One capsule every eight hours."

She turned to the printer, took the sheet, folded it in half, and finally, looked up to hand it over.

The woman reached out her hand.

The doctor looked at her.

And a single word escaped her lips in a broken breath: "Mom!"

TIME TO CATCH UP

The one who sleeps soundly wakes up to trouble.

During the pandemic, the world stopped. They didn't. Newlyweds, newly moved in, with newly unwrapped sheets and laptops. Two desks, one bed. Two offices in the same room. And at first, it was all honeymoon.

"You wanna...?" he whispered from his desk.

"I'm busy," she replied, eyes fixed on her screen.

The words still came warm, but sometimes there were breaks: brief, intense, like a too-strong coffee. He spoke of desire; she, of work. He spoke of love; she, of "catching up." Catching up... That phrase became her mantra, her shield. Catch up on the back-log, catch up on projects, fast-forward life to make more time. A time that, supposedly, never appeared.

He, more ardent, took refuge on hidden websites. She, the more level-headed one, grew ever more sullen and quiet. They stopped cooking, barely ate. Didn't go out, except for emergencies. Didn't talk, only what was necessary. Desire became a formula, caresses became memes, and pauses became notifications.

Until one night, she had an idea. He slept soundly, snoring. And when he slept, she was herself.

She worked. She caught up.

Oh, what a glorious moment—the screen, the uninterrupted time!

That's when the secret "solution" was born. Not poison, just rest.

And she used it. Once, twice, and again, diluted in the espresso he loved so much. He slept placidly while she stayed active, like a server with a perfect connection. To the nights, she added an afternoon nap; to the nap, a break. The pause became a constant.

But then both of them would awaken, relentless, hungry. He, like a baby, and that thing, like a beast.

The remedy had been worse than the disease. Each awakening brought with it a prouder, more stubborn, more prolonged erection. A body with the power of an Olympic athlete and the urgency of a lustful saint.

"Again?"

"Again."

She no longer put him to sleep just to rest from him, but to gain time between thrusts. The days and nights merged into one. He, in his mattress dent; she, in her chair, sightless and backless. He no longer worked; she no longer undressed.

And as the world outside reopened its doors, they remained locked in their new normal, between a bed and a desk, with their dreams put to sleep by two awakened devices: a glowing laptop and an erect penis.

LETTER TO MYSELF

Some truths don't fit in an envelope.

Dear Claudia,

I don't know how to start this letter. Maybe that's why it took me so long to write it—because every time I thought about doing it, a voice told me no, that you wouldn't understand, or that I was overreacting, or wasting my time. But staying silent is exhausting, and now I need to tell you a few things.

I don't want this to sound like a reproach—even if it is. Or a complaint—even if it hurts. I just want you to listen, the way I've always tried to listen to you.

I don't know when you became someone who has an opinion about everything and everyone. A busybody handing out unsolicited advice, the boss of what "should be done," and always first in line to point out other people's mistakes—of course. But when you mess up (and you sure do), it suddenly becomes "a learning experience that helped me grow." Do you even see it?

I'm tired of your selfies with motivational quotes you never apply to yourself, and the filters you hide behind. Your hollow lives on PikTok, filled with passive-aggressive jabs disguised as wisdom. That way you have of telling your problems as if the world owed you applause for surviving things that happen to everyone. Even the way you do your hair, dress, or walk… be more original.

And still, I love you. Or maybe I used to. I don't know. Because I've also laughed with you and cried with you, and sometimes I miss your voice when it's not around. But lately, when I hear you, I feel like you speak to be applauded, not to be understood.

I just wanted a friend, not a judge, not a lifestyle influencer for other people's lives.

And that's why I wrote this letter. Not posting it on social media, but writing it to you directly, in my own hand. Because if I didn't say it, I was going to lose you in silence. Maybe I'll still lose you—but at least this time, you'll have read what I have to say.

Sincerely,
Rosa María

The letter was folded with care, slipped into its envelope, sealed with a trembling, almost dry tongue, and dropped into the nearest mailbox.

Days went by. The mailbox remained empty—or full of useless, brightly colored ads.

Until one day, a letter arrived.

Judging by the thickness of the envelope, it was long. She grabbed it quickly and ran to the privacy of her room. She brushed her hair aside, sighed, and sat on the edge of her bed.

And then she noticed the front of the envelope.

Top left corner, the sender: Claudia (her friend's address).

In the center, the recipient: Rosa María (herself).

How confusing. It was her handwriting. It was her complaint.

It was her letter—mistakenly sent to herself.

She froze, cheeks flushing, as if someone had just shouted a truth at her. And there was no need to open it.

MERINGUE FLOWERS

This isn't about rights.
It's about opportunities.

In Front of the Mirror

I'm getting ready to go to the radio station, but I don't even know what I'm going to say. I've never been interviewed before!

I'm so nervous. Am I dressed okay? I already told my mom I didn't want a party; she insists on having a little get-together with the family and cutting the cake.

My mom is so thoughtful — she always surprises me with everything. She's so sweet! If it weren't for her... Ugh, that's enough! I don't want to cry today — but my makeup is already running.

"*Mami*, hand me the mascara, this thing's all smudged! And the lipstick too, *mima*!"

Where was I? Oh, right. I don't want parties. Not even when I turned fifteen did, I want one. That whole runway of frilly dresses...

"Thanks, *Mami*."

...it just feels so cheesy. Like we're stuck in some old-fashioned era! Not me — no way! Maybe I seem weird, but honestly I think I'm more grounded than my friends. Look at Magali — her family threw a huge party for her *quince*, and now they're neck-deep in debt. On top of that, she looked terrible in the photos — like a total mess. I just asked my mom for a good meal and that's it. And wow, did I feast!

We women aren't dolls to be dressed up and paraded around in some fake photo album.

I haven't seen my dad forever. Man, it's been ages! My breasts have even grown since then, and he's still nowhere to be found. The last time he sang me a *"japi beibi"*, he got so drunk he slapped my mom so hard she passed out on the floor. My grandma ended up kicking him out of the house. And good for her! He deserved it! Hitting my mom like that... She's been both mother and father to me and has busted her back working just to see me get ahead.

I'm not a little girl anymore — I get it. I've seen my mom cry her eyes out so many times.

When she was desperate, she'd throw herself on the bed and said she had a headache. As if I were stupid! She thought I didn't know it was because of my dad.

She'd whip up meals from nothing while that man was off lounging around. I remember once watching her making *fufú*, and it looked like she was seasoning it with tears. That night, he didn't come home.

Many times, she'd served my plate, and I'd ask if she had eaten. She'd always say yes—until one day I noticed there was nothing but the *raspa* left in the pot. From that day on, I made her sit and eat with me, and I'd get really grumpy if she refused. Who knows how many nights she went to bed hungry!

When things got really tough, Mom would open the closet and sit on the bed, just looking at her clothes. After a bit, she'd hand me a bag and ask me to go over to Tania's house or other friends to see if they wanted to buy anything. Slowly, she sold it all. Even the black velvet dress I loved so much, she let it go for a few pesos and a pound of rice. She emptied her closet to fill our plates. I can honestly say I was raised in my mom's dresses.

I was born on a day like today. Mom was the same age I am now, and honestly... she was a stunner. I've seen pictures of her, and I go crazy looking at the incredible figure she had, though girls back then were more developed than today's. Must be what they used to eat. With all these chemicals now, everything is so bad for us! Back then, everything was natural. Still, I can't complain—I've got my curves, and when I walk down the street, I stop traffic. Sometimes I even blush from the catcalls the *pepillos* throw my way. But guys get worked up over any old thing, they all look at us like they're starving. I'm one of those girls who's waiting for a man who truly loves me, who respects and values me for who I am. Do men like that even exist anymore?

Every year, my grandma and mom repeat the story of my birth like it's sacred. They say remembering is living again. But Lord... it's like a broken record! "My belly was huge," "I was always sleepy," "the cravings," "the checkups," "the swollen legs" ... What a routine! I was lucky to be born in a hospital, though, because Grandma says she was born in a bucket. Can you believe that?! Mom's belly was round like a beach ball, and everyone said it was a girl, because girls make their belly pointy. The poor thing nearly went crazy. Girls are more expensive than boys, everything's pink! But I was born in lean times—we didn't have a single cent to our name. If I had been a boy, I would've had plenty of clothes because my cousins passed down the *canastilla* from one to another. I think I was doomed to wear blue, although blue is my favorite color, and it matches my name. Ah... maybe that's why they named me this way! But they've never told me that.

"I'm coming, *mija!*"

My mom insists I eat lunch before I go, but when I'm nervous, I can't eat—I just throw it all up. Better when I get back. I wonder what they'll ask me. So much fuss over a cake!

"Where's the ID?!"

There's a saying: "Haste makes waste."

And my mom—once she gets something in her head... *Ñó*, that woman was born to compete. Well, maybe not her, but definitely me. They always say I was lazy even in the womb, that's why I didn't win the *canastilla*. And it was a good one —came with a crib and everything! After a month of being pampered, she'd been admitted and had a scheduled date. The doctors said I might be born on the night of the 7th. Everyone at home was biting their nails, but labor dragged on because she wasn't dilating. The contractions started at five in the afternoon. They kept taking her in and out, and me, just taking my sweet time inside. She was fighting like a beast, holding out as long as she could so she'd make it past midnight. You can't let a prize like that slip away! Who gives you a whole *canastilla* these days?

The biggest one a child in this town could ever get! Around eleven at night, her water broke, and they rushed her into the delivery room. She says that every time she pushed, she thought about the prize: the diapers (mmm!), the baby powder (mmm!), the cologne (mmm!), the little clothes (mmm!), the craaadle—hmmmmm!

When it's my turn, I'd rather get a C-section. Men should have to give birth, just so they know what it's like! I would've loved to see my dad pushing me out. Why is it always us women who get the worst part?

And then, our little champion found herself next to another pregnant woman—a strange competitor who didn't even look like she was in labor, walking in with a big smile like she was heading to an amusement park. And the rules were clear: it had to be a natural birth or no *canastilla*.

"*Mami*, what was the name of the one who got induced?!"

Ugh, Mónica! Every time I think of that Mónica, I get so mad… That thief! There's cheating everywhere. It shouldn't be the first baby born—it should be whoever's water breaks first. Or they should give something to every baby born that day. That woman must've pulled some strings, you could tell. They left my mom alone on the delivery table, pushing by herself, and rushed off to yank that another baby out. Totally rigged! Imagine, two women competing like it's a horse race!

"*Ay, Mami,* you should've pushed harder!"

With who? No one! With the mirror!

I'm rehearsing in case they ask me about it. She probably thinks I'm crazy, talking to myself.

If I hadn't taken so long, I would've been born first. By the time I poked my head out, they were already cutting the other girl's cord. And by the time they cut mine, she was already wearing a blouse from the *canastilla*.

She, the first girl born on March 8th, dressed in pink... and me, five minutes later, dressed in blue.

But it was cheating!

The good thing is, I've forgiven her. Besides, that *canastilla* doesn't even exist anymore. Though my mom was more heartbroken about losing the prize than about tearing. She argued with the doctors and cited all kinds of rules, but nothing worked.

And the worst part? She ended up breastfeeding that baby, just like a bunch of other babies in the nursery, because her boobs were about to burst and I wasn't hungry.

Life's little ironies! She takes my clothes, and I give her my milk. Everyone kept saying what a cute little boy she had, and she'd get mad and flash my toto so they could see I was definitely a girl. Of course, dressed in blue, who would've guessed! Oh wow, what a coincidence—today I'm wearing blue too. But hey, now you can clearly tell I'm a woman. At least I don't have to go around flashing anything anymore.

I'm sure this time I'll win the cake. I'm about to run to the radio station. After all, I've got my ID and I can prove I'm of age. Who would've thought?! Yesterday I was playing in the mud, and today I'm a young lady. Ay, but I can't imagine being a mom at my age! I hope when I have a baby, it's a boy—and by then, there's already an International Men's Day. I swear I'll win that *canastilla*, and if not, I've still got my cousins' hand-me-downs, which were once mine too and are still in perfect shape.

"Hey, *Ma*! 'Acuarela Mexicana' just started!" Right after that show comes the prize. My mom and I have waited eighteen years to get on the radio and win that cake.

"Yes, I'm coming!" Gosh, this woman is so impatient!

They say every year the cake ends up in the radio booth covered in meringue because nobody picks it up. What a waste! I think that cake's been waiting for me all these years. It's gotta be big—like three layers. I hope it has flowers! I love those little meringue flowers so, so much. That's my favorite part. *Ay*, I bet a ton of people are gonna hear me!

I'm so nervous! Okay, Azul, breathe. That cake is already yours! But... how am I gonna carry it home? I hadn't thought of that. Can you imagine if I drop it...

"Mami, how much does a cab from there cost?!" Geez, what a rip-off! People act like money grows on trees! But it doesn't matter, it's better to make sure it gets here in one piece. It won't fit on the kitchen table—we'll have to put it on the bed and throw a mosquito net over it, because this swarm of flies is out of control...

"*Es mi orgullo haber nacido...*" That song gets to me every time. It's like Mexico already knew my story when they wrote it. Okay, I'm ready.

"*Mami*, what time is it?"

WHAT?! Run, girl! We're almost out of time!

In front of the mirror again

Goodness, I need spiritual cleansing or something! I swear I hurried! History repeats itself. Before "Acuarela Mexicana" even ended, we ran out the door, and no matter how fast we ran—I missed the cake. The smart ones live off the fools, and the fools off their foolishness. What are five minutes, girl?! Five minutes is nothing! I swear, you couldn't even see my feet—I was flying!

But that cake wasn't for me. Just like so many other things in life. Who would've guessed it? Of course... we're the same age... "Mami, how could you forget about Mónica's daughter?!" That's right: my milk-sister snatched the cake from me. By five minutes. Just five tiny minutes!

We both arrived, sweaty and out of breath, and they told us another birthday girl had just walked in. Eighteen years waiting, and I'm left high and dry!

Mami always used to say, "When you turn eighteen, I'll take you to the radio station so you can win the cake."

It's the cake they give to the first girl who turns eighteen on International Women's Day and shows up at the station right after the program "Acuarela Mexicana." They even interview her, live, so everyone hears the lucky one. It's a sweet little tradition, and it would've made me popular in the neighborhood.

What a joke. Me, talking to the mirror—while she steals the whole show. She's the one speaking into the mic, while I'd already eaten the meringue flowers in my imagination.

OUT OF THE WATER

Don't swim against the current.
Dive in.

Riba had been born with a severe condition, and from an early age, he suffered the rejection and mockery of other children. His parents sought to give him a happy life and tried to provide ideal spaces for his development, but Riba was not like the other boys. He required special care: he couldn't be exposed to the sun or dust, his clothes had to be light and soft, and creams had to be constantly applied, as his scaly skin would get irritated, and at times, the situation became critical. He had a strange way of breathing, taking in air in great gulps, like a party balloon. He loved to run in the rain and splash around chasing frogs. When he went out on the street, some damning finger would always point at him. He was the target of the crudest and most painful discrimination, as if he didn't belong to this world or as if God had made a mistake in placing him in his parents' arms. However, the Fish-Boy, as they called him, was the most desired child in the world, the fulfilled dream of an elderly couple.

Today, all of that is in the past. He is now like the others and can go here and there without tiring. No longer a stranger, he is a fish in water. He has friends with whom he jumps, plays, and laughs like other children. No one points at him or sees him as a weirdo. He has a great ability to move, and his skin is now shiny and beautiful.

His family went on a camping trip, bringing everything needed to have a good time. The women were quick to light the fire, perfuming the air with their heady spices, while a succulent stew was already bubbling in the mysterious cauldron. The men decided to inflate their inner tubes and head to the river. With the water running high, they could launch themselves from the waterfall without too much risk. Riba's mother was reluctant to let him go, but his father believed that an experience of pure adrenaline would be good for him and convinced her. He held him in his right arm while the raft hung from his other.

The river was deeper than ever, its water cool and crystal clear despite the recent rains. The current was strong, carrying them at its whim along the frantic, roaring channel. The splashing and laughter crowned the adventure, easing the little ones' fright. Riba was enjoying it, but he felt he had to cling to the raft with all his might while his father captained the unhinged vessel.

"Move your little feet, Riba!" his father, the loving admiral of their craft, told him, perhaps because of the novice's visible shock.

The Fish-Boy began to feel at home, the protagonist of his own journey. At times, he felt the innocent nibbles of some mischievous fish on his legs. They say that water reclaims its place sooner or later, to die where it must, and Riba, at such a young age, was experiencing something important. He had reached the key moment of his story, swimming between two hopelessly opposed worlds. He was being born that day for a second time.

That's how joyful and entertaining the race of inflatables had been when, just like that, the boy slipped from the flotilla. He slid out from the wide ring that held him and, as if pulled by a mysterious force, ended up at the bottom of the river. As he sank, he could feel the vivid caress of the deep current, an applause of waning voices growing ever fainter, and a light twinkling restlessly among the agitated feet he had left on the surface. The world down below had a different color. Riba trembled at the number of new things appearing before his eyes and began to worry about returning to his father. The air was starting to run out, but he didn't feel uncomfortable; he waited patiently in that magical place, sure that his father would come for him.

Up above, the men no longer knew what to try. His father went down and came up with the desperation of the stream itself, failing to find him amidst voices, shouts, and anguished wails. Down below, in some strange place, the Fish-Boy waited, resigned.

The time came to make a decision. Riba had to awaken and begin his own rescue. He started to move his body, driven by the sole idea of peeking above that shimmering fabric on which his father floated. His effort began to pay off, and he emerged little by little. The shouts and cries grew louder as he neared the surface. His father searched for him frantically, bellowing his name. Riba rose like an expert and, popping his little head out, began to shout as he struggled to stay afloat. But all the noise and confusion seemed to be the reason why neither his father nor the others could hear or see him. While he kept calling them forcefully, everyone seemed to ignore him.

He had already found a way to move from side to side without trouble; you could say he swam like a natural. He took the opportunity to get closer and, with surprise, found that even when he was right beside him, gently nipping at his body, the man who until then had been his father continued to search for who-knows-what in the turbulent waters, not realizing that what he was so desperately seeking was right next to him.

"Dad, I'm here! Dad! Dad!" he shouted, but the more he did, the more he was ignored.

One of his cousins seemed to see him and, with the same damning finger as before, pointed at him while letting out a cry of childish wonder:

"Look, Daddy, there's a beautiful fish over there!"

When night fell, the men left, and with them, his father, who for the first time had left him alone. From then on, his life was different, his home was different, his world was now different. Today, he cruises the waters like any other. Today, he has a life, and every time someone approaches, he jumps enthusiastically by their side, welcoming them. It is these moments that evoke his first family, those occasions when he remembers that once, he was out of the water.

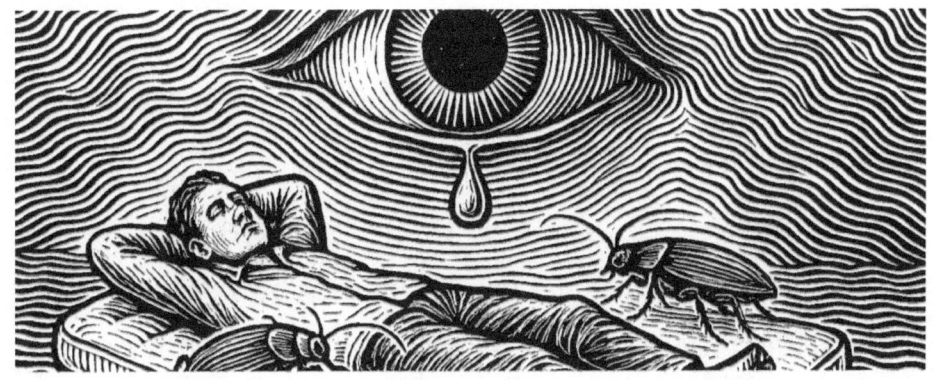

PSYCHEDELIC EYES

You saw me.
I saw myself.

A coldness chilled me to the bone the moment I entered. A shiver ran down my spine, and I felt my hands and feet grow numb. My mouth went dry. My lips burned and swelled. Everything around me was darkness, but little by little, I began to make out shadows and flashes of light, from which strange figures emerged.

I was met by a monster whose glowing eyes contrasted with the cave. I simply backed away, not lingering on my emotions. It had an elongated head, a large mouth, and claws that stretched like shadows. It wanted to catch me in a strange, almost affectionate way. I tried to escape. I ran slowly, heavily, like in a dream. Its claws stretched like chewing gum, grazing me without ever quite reaching me.

I passed through a labyrinth of sightlines, fleeing the monster's grasp. In the end, I found myself climbing an infinite staircase. As I ascended, my body grew lighter, as if it were no longer entirely mine. I kept climbing as if by inertia, and then... I fell onto a soft, springy mattress that cushioned my fall.

I was floating on a dense, white, shoreless river. I let myself be carried away. In the distance, I saw two enormous, luminous eyes, fixed on me, as if black space itself were watching me. They blinked, and I was hypnotized. I put my arms behind my head and floated on that mattress, upon that glowing river, as if it were all part of a liquid performance, observing those eyes that never stopped watching me, without any threat.

The eyes separated, turned vertical, and sprouted cockroach legs. They moved clumsily, out of sync, getting closer. A wave of nausea hit me. They climbed onto the mattress and began to touch me. An itch spread over my whole body, and I wanted to escape by throwing myself into the water.

I emerged. There was a total silence. Just a faint, rhythmic dripping, as if something were escaping from me.

The coat rack, piled high with clothes, stood like a motionless monster.

The cockroaches feasted on the nacho cheese, oblivious to everything.

Spilled beer spread across the carpet, reaching the flip-flops.

A wet line still traced a slow path from my eyelids to my chin. I had been crying.

And then, I discovered the forbidden cigarette, smoldering on the arm of the chair.

TIMBERMAN

Not every shortcut leads you astray.

Ivan's father was a despicable, brutally absolute male. A broad-backed animal with a gravelly voice, firm hands, and a perpetually grim, stone-like face that seemed to cast a sentence with his every step. When he appeared, he dominated the space; when he breathed, it felt like a punishment. He smelled of tobacco, dry earth, and the fermented sweat of his armpits—the kind of scent carried only by men who don't apologize for being men. When he spoke, the walls seemed to tense up; when he yelled, the spoons trembled in their drawers. He would settle in the living room like an invisible totem, and when he fell silent, the wars would cease.

And yet, he knew how to kiss his wife's forehead. He knew how to touch her hand, the curves of her body over her apron, with an unexpected tenderness. He knew when to keep silent and when to fix his gaze as if laying down the law.

Ivan's mother loved him madly. She said it without shame: "I have an angel in the living room and a devil in the bed." Ivan would recoil, avert his gaze, terrified.

Everything about his father was large, firm, unquestionable. Even his silences were judgmental, as if he might crush everything with his shadow.

He had learned to live carefully: not to show too much, not to say too much, and above all, not to be in the way. Because Ivan was also a man and felt like a man. He liked his youthful body. He looked at himself in the mirror with satisfaction; he shaved with dignity and pride. He enjoyed watching his muscles take shape, how the hair grew on his chest, and how his legs and arms tensed when he went to the gym. He took selfies without guilt. He liked the shape of his neck, his jaw, the color of his skin, and the smell of his underwear. He didn't want to be a woman; he wasn't interested in costumes or extremes. He felt like a man and was happy to be one.

But he liked men: the strong bodies, the deep voices, the firm gaze of another who knew how to hold him. He didn't experience it as a contradiction, but as a truth. He knew, however, that in his house, that truth could not be shared. His father wouldn't understand it. He would kill him. He would see it as a deviation, a sin, a weakness; as something to be corrected, cured, or punished. He was a religious man. That's why Ivan stayed silent.

That night, Ivan was twenty-one. He had been gifted a car with low mileage. His mother slept soundly, without a stir, and his father was gone, without exception.

Ivan had a desire he could no longer keep quiet. He no longer wanted to imagine; he wanted to live it. He wanted body, flesh, encounter, risk. He had spent weeks exploring on Timber, scrolling through connected profiles, discarding and saving favorites. His type was clear: he wanted to be held by someone who would pierce through everything—the body, skin, fear.

And he found the one. No face was shown, but there was a manly arm, tan and well-groomed. Forties. Discreet. Available. "No limits," the bio said. They chatted briefly. Everything fit. The encounter would be quick, in a secluded, dimly lit public park, inside the car. They agreed to meet at the far end.

Ivan put on cologne, a new outfit he'd been saving for a special occasion and took two shots to loosen his anxiety. He left without a sound. He drove with a crooked smile, his chest pounding, his skin tingling with expectation, and a half-erection. He felt handsome and brave. This was his moment.

"Where are you?" he wrote.

"Come all the way to the back. My car is the silver one", was the reply.

The car didn't draw attention. He approached and tapped on the window. The door opened. Inside, a naked body was waiting for him: taut skin, leather, rings, the posture of a lion tamer. The man of his dreams.

"Shit."

It was his father.

UNRECOGNIZED CHARGE

Everything has a price.

J ulio was a man with a clear conscience. His salary, hard-
earned at the workshop, was converted into hard cash.
He saved carefully and spent moderately, for he knew the
value of every dollar.

That's why, when the bank denied him a small loan to
upgrade his tools, citing a low "credit score," he felt a pang of
injustice. Him, who had never owed a cent to anyone.

His friends, on the other hand, swam in those waters with
an enviable ease. Juan, Andrés, and Ricardo would toss around
numbers as if discussing the weather: their scores, their gold

cards, their interest-free installment plans. Julio would celebrate with them, a sincere smile on his face, though something ached inside. He was outside the club.

He decided to get in. He looked for the door on the internet, where words like "Interest Rates," "yields," "APR," and "leverage" floated like pieces of a puzzle. His friends were no help. Juan said, "I just pay the bill, that's it." Andrés talked about firewalls, secure gateways, and antivirus software with fancy names. Ricardo, more mystical, spoke of DeFi and a future without banks while paying the tab with his cashback credit card.

The revelation came in the grocery store line, between eggs and toilet paper. A woman, without knowing it, opened up the world to him: "I got the 'Oportum' store card, bought the mattress, paid it off on time, and boom! That darn score went right up."

Julio, clinging to that wisdom from the common folk, applied for his department store card, bought the hammer drill he needed, and paid each monthly installment like a good deed for a soul in need.

And it worked. The magic number began to move, timidly at first, then with confidence. One day, a letter arrived: "Congratulations. You have been pre-approved for our Sterling Bank Platinum card with a credit limit of $500." He hadn't done anything new; he just paid his bills. Some mysterious algorithm had decided he was now worthy. He felt important. He started checking the banking app like someone consulting their horoscope: balance, closing date, due date, minimum payment. His score would go up ten points, down two, up seven. It was a numerical roller coaster, but one with power over his mood. He could finally say it: he was part of the club.

Until he saw it. Between the internet bill and the grocery purchase, one line stopped him: "ROBO – $99.99." His heart raced. "It must be an error," he thought with a borrowed sense of calm.

He called the bank. After the hold music, Agent One listened with catalog-grade courtesy: "We understand your frustration, Mr. Pérez. Please allow me to transfer you to our Disputes department."

Agent Two, his patience measured in minutes, instructed him: "You must fill out form CSD-723A. Download it from our website. Attach a copy of your ID, proof of address, and a written statement detailing the facts." Julio downloaded the form; it was like deciphering a language invented by vengeful bureaucrats.

His friends, once again, were no help. Juan sighed, "Happened to me. They got me for 50 bucks. Nothing you can do. The juice isn't worth the squeeze."

Andrés suggested, "Phishing! Have you scanned your computer? Use 'CyberWall Ultra,' I'll send you the link, it's on sale."

Ricardo, smiling condescendingly, said, "Told you. Banks are fossils. Join the crypto world. I'm already out of the Matrix."

Julio sent the documents and waited. Days turned into weeks. He called again. Agent Three told him, "Your case is in the final stage of review. Please be patient, we will contact you. Estimated time: fifteen to thirty business days."

Agent Four informed him, "We can't find your initial request. Could you resend it? And please report to a branch with a handwritten letter." His score was teetering like a Jenga tower.

One night, filled with insomnia and rage, he searched online. A forum popped up: "HELP! Unrecognized charges from 'Remote Optimized Billing Office LLC' (ROBO LLC)." There were dozens of stories identical to his. The same powerlessness. One comment was a godsend: "Use the Consumer Protection Code XR-45. It's a miracle."

Julio called again. He said it without a tremor in his voice: "I know my rights. Consumer Protection Code XR-45."

There was a silence, and the agent's tone changed. "Please allow me a moment. I'm going to review your case personally."

Two days later, the charge was reversed. Julio exhaled. He had done it. He had won.

Weeks later, he checked his statement again. The $99.99 charge was gone, and his score had gone up by one point. He smiled, but his smile quickly faded. A little further down, a new line item jumped out:

"Dispute Resolution Fee: $14.99 (With Loyal Customer Discount)."

CONFESSIONS OF A CAT

You enjoy the play from your seat...
until the curtain falls.

My observation post is unbeatable, here on the windowsill, where the morning sun spills like warm honey. My white coat, a testament to my passage, clings to the texture of the armchair, to the frayed velvet of the curtain.

The glass, sometimes veiled by the breath of the night, is the border of my kingdom. From it, I contemplate the whirlwind outside. My feline eyes remain active, hunting the prey offered by this incessant spectacle. An insatiable hunger for the living, for that restless swarm of beings out there, keeps me alert. My gaze, sharp and patient, follows the erratic flight of a disoriented butterfly, the lazy fall of an autumn leaf.

A comfortable tremor, a deep and steady hum, is born in my chest when the sun finally conquers my cushion. It is one of the few certainties, this warmth that seeps deep inside. From here, I judge the coming and going of those young creatures with their shrieks that pierce the air and movements that defy stillness, and then the adults, with urgency etched on their features. If I were free, if I could run after them, catch those flies buzzing against the glass, those rebellious birds that dare to challenge my quietude, play with that caterpillar venturing along the outer frame, feel again the hair-raising fear of a dog catching up to me... How predictable they are in their haste!

My large ears, mobile and attentive to the slightest whisper, turn toward the scratching of branches against the wall. A colder puff of air slips through a crack and makes me curl up tighter, seeking to preserve the heat. I would like to reunite with my own kind as before, around this armchair and this window, but this glass defines my dreams and separates me from the world.

The parade is a custom. The faces change out there, but here, routine is an anchor. Anonymous hands offer me caresses; the water bowl is always full, the food appears without a word being spoken, sometimes accompanied only by a distant murmur from my caretakers. Thus, these fleeting presences fulfill their ritual. If it weren't for this window that offers me the world and for the old ball of yarn that enthralls me thread by thread, I don't know what would become of these long hours. I entertain myself by observing everything from my windowsill, unraveling threads with playful swipes of my paw.

And still, here I am. The dust of years accumulates under these chipped claws. A purr of memories assails my mind; longing grooms me. An oblique ray of light offers a silent spectacle that can absorb my attention for stretches that, to others, would be an eternity. I am a forgotten little animal.

Today, the light shrinks earlier. a coldness I know well creeps silently up from the edges of the frame. Time to turn in. My descent is no longer the agile leap of yesteryear, that simple impulse to leave the windowsill. Dexterity is now a distant echo. I seek, with calculated slowness, the polished wooden arm of the chair that someone, long ago, had the thoughtfulness to pull up to this window. A cry, more air than sound, escapes me as I fall. The body resists but yields with the slowness of a receding tide.

I am old now.

Before, I was the girl who ran in that park that I now barely distinguish through the fogged glass and the years. I was the young woman who hurriedly boarded the bus straight to work, feeling the pulse of the city in every puff of smoke. I was also the mother who pushed her son on the swing in the backyard, pushing dreams that flew high. All of that is gone, like water through my fingers. Now, I am just an old woman, with feline eyes, saying goodbye to life from the window of my room in this forgotten nursing home.

THE FLY AND THE CHAMELEON

Not everything is digestible.
Some things are savored, chewed, and then spat out.

A particular stench, that of promises emanating from the system's rot, seduced the fly, making her dream of taking flight, of a definitive escape. Her existence was spent in a modest but stable job, among mountains of cans she had to sort, stack, and display with care. It was a fly's work for an ant's salary. Garbage. It stunk.

The weight of routine was compounded by the anguish of her legal status; everything she was and possessed teetered constantly under the threat of possible deportation.

Amid this anxiety, a dream resonated, the vibrant echo of a promise: "Stop being a fly, you could fly higher, be a bumblebee. Don't consume, generate. We can help you. Go to..."

And so, the chameleon's long tongue stretched until it reached her workplace. As she arranged the cold cans, she heard the news: things could change, a better future was possible, but signatures were needed. If the candidate won, he would support the working people, make the nation great, and grant work visas. He promised an oasis of abundance during a chaotic and violent world; they would no longer have to sneak in or invade borders but would enter with their heads held high. With permission. It was the dream longed for by every immigrant.

"That's the guy," the fly told herself, feeling an irrepressible urge. "I need to go; I need to add my signature. I want to participate."

She arrived at the indicated place: a building of austere modernity, with four walls and a door, the bare minimum. It was painted a deep red. The fly was also wearing red that day; she had "put on the jersey" eager to be seen as part of the movement. Inside, in the simple and sober office, the red chameleon received her with a kind and seductive smile. He unfurled a politician's flowery speech, wrapping her in his tongue, savoring her without quite digesting her, for he only craved her signature.

He then extended the paper, an immaculately white sheet. She signed, fully convinced.

"We are changing the present, building a new future, making history," the chameleon proclaimed.

And the fly left there feeling the budding of new wings, filled with hope.

The chameleon won. Slowly, but surely, he reached the summit of popular acceptance, and from there he began to change the present, but also to erase the past, building a future of great depression.

The fly, meanwhile, continued to rummage among the cans. Her beautiful dream of being a bumblebee had dissolved in the saliva of that triumphant lizard, and her legal status, far from being secured, continued to teeter dangerously. The chameleon had not only taken her signature; now, from his position of power, he imposed decrees that turned her into a criminal, an invader of the system. He took away the bond that had once given her a respite, revoked her work permit, and with it, stole her peace.

It was then that she heard a flutter, perhaps of news or of gossip, an insistent buzzing among the shelves. Another fly told her: "A lawyer. There's a legal umbrella, I already applied. The process is a pain, yes, but the law is the law."

A new spark ignited. "Fly," she told herself, "Escape this garbage heap of cans." And once more, the sweet, corrupt stench of the system led her back to the chameleon's lair.

The same building now painted a boring gray. Inside, the gray chameleon waited for her in the same desolate environment, where only the pristine white of a sheet of paper stood out.

"Article X of the law," he recited with an imperturbable face, "under the 'so-and-so' provision, gives you the opportunity to appeal."

"I don't have much money," the fly whispered.

"Don't worry," the being replied, "our notaries are as qualified as any lawyer."

The fly felt herself being savored, drowned in the sweet, sticky saliva of her captor. She signed and, once again, was catapulted to her fate. Soon, the cans began to fall from her hands like a bad omen. "I've been scammed," the certainty hit her. The notary fled with all the money. Her fears were brutally confirmed; the legal umbrella had closed, and the storm had caught her.

Shortly after, she was fired from her job.

"You'll always be welcome here," they told her with cold courtesy, "once you sort out your situation."

Tears flooded her large fly eyes. She began a flightless, aimless march into the unknown.

Goodbye to the cans, goodbye to the precarious stability. Her credit card debt grew at a dizzying pace. The rent was due soon, lurking. She needed to negotiate.

No longer with desire or hope, her weak wings, almost by inertia, carried her back to that building, whose door, ominously, was already open.

The blue chameleon received her. His face was now a calculating blue, like a frozen sea; his saliva, once sweet, had become bitter and complex.

"Your situation is complicated," the chameleon hissed. "The numbers don't add up, you're in the red everywhere. But we could make an exception. You have a good history."

He spun her around on his deceiving tongue, a vertigo of figures and clauses. In the end, exhausted and confused, the fly accepted the deal to pawn her debt. She signed and fled that blue building like someone escaping the jaws of a predator.

And that is how she became homeless. She then discovered a world to which she seemed to have always been destined, falling into the bottomless pit of desperation and hunger. Now she knew that down there, flies and pestilence abounded, and that the cold contempt of others killed them slowly.

She no longer went anywhere with her own free will. This time, they came for her. A long, thorny tongue, visible and brutal, dragged her through the streets, displaying her shame, and brought her to that building that now sported a poisonous green. She no longer trusted his saliva, which now dripped shamelessly between sharp teeth, bathing the paper that, once again, she had to sign.

"We're going to help you," the green chameleon said with a sly grin. "No strings attached. It's a matter of public health and social justice. A matter of public order." His speech was a grotesque parody. "We'll give you what you need. What do you need? We have food, clothes, and water. Lots of donations."

So, the fly signed. Not a commitment, but a consent, an explicit permission for them to act. She left there without wings, completely stripped, like a crawling insect. But, for the first time, she left with something tangible: a loaf of stale bread, a frayed blanket, a bottle of no-name water. And a number. A label. A file. She was now officially on assistance.

The heat inside the old, pawned van was intense, a microwave disintegrating his emotions. His bathing suit was already dry after leaving the pool at the apartment complex where he once lived. He got up with an effort, abandoned that den of misery in the parking lot of the supermarket where he once worked, and walked away. He was leaving everything behind: his van, his broken wings. He took a few hesitant steps on the burning asphalt. He saw the can of expired tuna from the donation that he had thrown onto the pavement hours before, now swarming with frantic flies. He smiled, and bitter tears snaked down his dirty face. He drew back and kicked the can with all his might, sending it flying.

Then, he crossed the border on foot, under the infernal sun, in the opposite direction, heading back home.

THE COFFEE OF CONCORD

The word can build or destroy.
War is unleashed on the tongue;
peace, by binding it, or at least, by reining it in.

The city air vibrated with a mix of solemnity and discreet celebration. It was Mestre's Day. The streets were adorned with garlands woven from laurel and olive leaves, and soft instrumental melodies emanated from public loudspeakers, occasionally interrupted by the reading of a memorable passage from the great strategists of the word.

Away from the epicenter of the official ceremonies, Roy was opening his shop. The old man, whose asymmetrical smile and slightly drooping eyelid were the visible map of a conflict—his last service-related injury—exuded a serene charm, like that of a patient grandfather. The shop was modest, painted in cream tones, and smelled of freshly brewed coffee and the thousand stories held within the second-hand objects that populated its shelves. A small sign with meticulous calligraphy read: "Good Thrift. All proceeds to the House of Sunflowers (Orphans of the Discord). Mestres: 50% Off, today and always."

The bell on the door tinkled and in walked Alejandro, a young exchange student with a backpack slung over his shoulder and a gaze full of the curiosity of one exploring a foreign world. He came from the Farlands, a nation that flourished in quiet peace, without the historical need to have forged Concords.

"Welcome, young man," the old man greeted, his eyes shining with genuine kindness. "A busy day to be opening, but charity knows no holiday. Coffee? It's on the house."

"Thank you, sir, that's very kind of you," Alejandro replied, accepting the steaming cup. "I've been observing the celebrations. In my land, we don't have Mestres. It's all very impressive, and I see you offer them a permanent discount. I'd like to understand more about them, about these 'wars' you speak of. Mr....?"

"Meyer," Roy answered, gesturing for him to take a seat. "What's your name?"

"My name is Alejandro."

"To understand..." Roy murmured. "That's a good starting point. A seed.

You see, Alejandro, I don't know why men have always fought. It seems a primitive impulse, a matter of survival more than supremacy. My mother used to say that when you're small, you must bare your teeth with rage to be respected. The strength of the face, the one that persuades or intimidates, has been more decisive than the strength of the arm. Even great monsters of humanity were, physically, short men with bad tempers," the old man said, clenching his jaw as he showed off his impeccable dentures. They both laughed. After a pause for a sip of coffee, he continued: "Deep down, wars arise from an inferiority complex, or the opposite.

"The nature of war evolved, of course. From sticks and stones to arrows and spears; then fire, swords, cannons, automatic weapons, drones, viruses... a crescendo of long-range horror. After the Great Silence—the global disarmament that nearly wiped us off the map—man needed to keep warring, but the weapons had changed. Now, the battle would be fought with words. And there, my boy, the Concords were born.

"They were, and some still are, the soldiers of the word. Their ammunition is the words themselves, chosen with precision.

Their weapons are books: history, philosophy, the art of empathy. And their training ground is the library.

"Every Concord's training, Alejandro, begins with a coffee in the library. That's how mine began, so many years ago. I've forgotten many things, but not that first sip. Coffee, they told us, helps the brain, fights oxidation, awakens consciousness, and fosters concord.

"It's a small ritual before immersing oneself in the study of how words can build or destroy worlds. From that first coffee, the path is long. First as an Aspirant or Sub-Concord, then a Neo-Concord in the field, later a Concord, the full professional. Some reach the rank of Sum-Concord, and finally, a few of us become a Mestre, an emeritus title, post-service. But don't be fooled," Roy's voice grew deeper, "it's a hard, hard battle. We fight against disinformation, demagoguery, fear.

"I remember a campaign in the Southeastern Province where an isolationist movement was poisoning the population. We spent weeks there, listening, talking, refuting lies with facts. It was exhausting. Every night, you felt your soul was empty, only to refill it with hope the next day."

The Mestre paused, unconsciously touching his afflicted cheek. "These marks aren't just from time; they are from those battles. The constant pressure, the responsibility... the body and mind suffer for it. Extreme stress-induced paralysis, they call this. I've seen Mestres with tremors, with broken voices, with exhausted hearts. These are the silent wounds of this war. That's why Mestre's Day is an honor, yes, but also a reminder that our active service has ceased because we need our minds to rest."

Alejandro had listened in overwhelmed silence, his coffee forgotten. "So..." he murmured, "the injuries you speak of aren't just metaphors. Mestre Meyer... is this war necessary? I was born into peace; we don't have an army of peacemakers like you do. Perhaps I am drinking a coffee I haven't roasted or ground myself."

Roy looked at him with profound understanding. "Necessary is a heavy word, Alejandro. What alternative did we have when we saw the poison of discord re-emerging? We decided to stand in the way, and the price is high. And as for your coffee, you've touched a very raw nerve. Few are those who cultivate every bean of the peace they enjoy. Often, that peace is a commodity sustained by unseen hands. Your land, where peace is the air you breathe, is an ideal. But ask yourself, how is it maintained? Is it self-sustaining, or are the verbal storms perhaps contained by armies like ours, acting as lightning rods? Nothing exists in a vacuum, Alejandro. Understanding that is the beginning of a very great wisdom."

Time seemed to stand still. Finally, Alejandro stood up and let his gaze wander around the shop, stopping on a thick volume with a worn, blue cover: Beasts' Legacy.

"Mestre Meyer, how much is this book?"

"Fifteen dollars, it's a special edition," the Mestre replied. "Although that, my boy, is just its price, not its cost. The cost is on every page. It is an arduous journey, but worth every step." Then, he added with a special glint in his good eye, "But for you, today, it will only be $7.50."

Alejandro looked up, surprised. "Fifty percent off? Is that also for Mestre's Day?"

Roy shook his head gently. "Not exactly, and yes. It's because I believe that today, with your questions, your sensitivity, and that metaphor about your coffee, you have taken your first step toward the Concord. You have begun to see the invisible threads, to sense the price of harmony. And that deserves to be recognized. Consider this book one more small tool for that path you may have, without knowing it, already begun to walk."

Alejandro, his heart tight with gratitude, paid for the relic. "I don't know how to thank you, Mestre Meyer. For the coffee, for the book... for everything."

"There's nothing to thank me for, Alejandro," the old man replied, placing the money in a simple wooden box. "It has been a pleasure. It's good to know there are young men like you, with open hearts and minds. Have a good journey, Alejandro. And may the peace you know continue to accompany you, but may you now see it with new eyes. The doors of Good Thrift will always be open."

Back in his homeland, amidst the greenery and calm he had always taken for granted, Alejandro opened the tome of Beasts' Legacy. On the first page, he discovered an elegant, slightly trembling handwriting in sepia ink, which read:

To you, who dare to taste a coffee from a distant harvest:

May its flavor inspire you to seek the root of
your own peace. And to care for it.

—RM.

RECYCLING

The one who writes it, speaks it.
The one who reads it, knows it.
But the one who tells it, holds the power.

5:04 AM

The alarm was an insistent, digital hum. Simón swatted in the darkness until he silenced it. The air purifier rattled discreetly beside his bed. PM2.5: 18 µg/m³. Moderate. The night air had grown stagnant. He sat up. On his side of the mattress, the same groove as always. In the bathroom, he used the last drop of shampoo from a plastic bottle with a sophisticated design.

5:32 AM

The kitchen was dimly lit by the small bulb on the coffee maker. Simón inserted the capsule. A click, a hiss, and the dark, reddish drip of 'Morning Intense' into his favorite mug. The city was just beginning to stir.

6:17 AM

He lit his first cigarette by the window. The smoke alarm was broken, so nothing forced him to go outside. As he was getting dressed, a spark jumped and burned the sleeve of the shirt he had just put on. "Occupational hazard." He sighed, left it on the bed, and chose another. The smell of stale smoke was a ghost that lived in his closet.

6:45 AM

Alone in his old car, he joined the vermilion river of wheels and lights flowing toward the city. Red was the route marked on the GPS, red were the traffic lights at every corner, red were the AQI levels. The smoke escaping from his tailpipe was a bit denser and darker than the others.

7:00 AM - 5:00 PM

The day at the auto parts store was a succession of calls, serial numbers, and the metallic scent of parts and solvent from the adjoining workshop. He printed three quotes that the customer ultimately didn't take. For lunch, he heated up an instant soup in the small office microwave and ate its contents in ten minutes, barely tasting it.

5:45 PM

On his way home, he stopped at the supermarket. A harsh, cold light flooded the infinite aisles, a sustained and overwhelming winter microclimate. He bought milk, more coffee, and some juicy-looking mangoes. At the checkout, the employee, with an automatic gesture, bagged his items in six plastic bags.

6:30 PM

At home, he unpacked the groceries. One of the mangoes already had a soft, dark spot. He left them on the countertop and had a pre-cooked meal from a tray for dinner. Afterward, he turned on the smart diffuser, adding a few drops of his favorite essential oil to create the relaxing ambiance he so enjoyed.

8:00 PM

He sat in front of his large television while working on the sketches for his remodeling project. Frustrated, he crumpled several sheets of paper and left them on the table.

10:30 PM

Before taking out the trash and going to bed, he checked the mail in his mailbox: junk mail, flyers, bills. One envelope caught his eye. Plain, white, no stamp. Just his name, "Simón," marked with a few smudges. He opened it. It read:

Simón Pérez:

You get up at five o'clock sharp. The alarm from an old cell phone you threw out days ago is still active in a landfill somewhere, too. Your coffee is 'Morning Intense.' You smoke a pack a day of the filtered kind. Sometimes, the ash burns your clothes and the soles of your sneakers. You're a size 8. Simón, Simón... so bad at the helm... you ran a red light on Tuesday. Your car is pure pollution. You care a lot about the quality of the air you breathe at home, sparing no expense on purifiers, but the car you drive alone every morning won't pass its emissions test anymore.

You work at the auto parts store from seven to five. Sometimes you bring parts home. You're not extravagant with groceries, but your mangoes rot, and I don't understand why they sometimes come in three bags. Your diet is based on microwaved food. You're very clean; your trash smells more like bleach and disinfectant than food. Though the chewing gum never makes it, only the wrappers. You're tired, you take sedatives, and some of them slip out among the scraps. Be careful, the instructions on their containers warn of possible side effects.

Your remodeling project is frustrating you. You have the biggest TV in the neighborhood; its box is comfortable but cold, they don't make them like they used to. I'm sure you enjoy good shows in a citrus-scented room. Your electric bill is very high. You make good money.

It's been a year since I've known anything about her, not since that last sanitary pad. But that's none of my business. I only know what you throw away. And from the scraps, I know you like flannel pajamas; they're very warm.

I'm going to sleep now. Right when the light from your bedside lamp stops illuminating the dumpster.

Sincerely,

Julia.

SAINT ELENA

Turn your problem into an opportunity.

For the first time in years, perhaps in his entire life, Juan crossed the threshold of his home feeling the weight of his own soul, and not the fury that made it invisible. He was coming home sober. Not just from alcohol, but from rage.

The door closed behind him with a soft click, and he noticed the felt doormat with its autumn motif that Elena had placed at the entrance. It smelled of cinnamon and damp earth. The sharp tinkling of the oriental wind chimed hanging from the frame, a sound that had so often been the trigger for a shout, now seemed to him a light, almost calming melody.

He was quiet. He felt broken, like an imploded building, but in the center of the rubble, he sensed a strange lightness. Elena was sitting at the kitchen table, her back to him. Her shoulders were tense. She was eating an apple with small, silent bites. When he entered, the faint creak of his footsteps on the wooden floor made her stop. She turned her head slowly. Her eyes, red and swollen, looked at him with a familiar fear, but the sweetness of her mouth had not been broken.

"Are you hungry?" she asked, her voice barely a whisper.

He didn't answer. He approached from behind, his steps softer now. She remained still, her gaze fixed ahead, the apple forgotten in her hand. Her entire body trembled visibly when she felt his presence at her back, perhaps expecting another episode—a blow, a word like a whiplash. But the aggression didn't come. Juan bent at the waist, bringing his face close to her neck. He smelled her. She smelled of flower shampoo and the salty fear of her sweat. And then, he kissed the nape of her neck. Softly. Slowly. Wetly.

A sob escaped Elena's throat, a sound that was half relief, half disbelief. She rose from her hard seat, turned to him, and in a quick, desperate movement, she threw her arms around his neck, hiding her face in his shoulder. And then they cried. Both. He, like a beaten dog that finally receives a caress, like a child stripped of his innocence too soon. He cried for his dead. He cried for her, for Elena, for the terror he had made her feel just moments before.

And as his body shook with spasms, a word came from his mouth, fragmented, with a strange accent: "For... give... me."

Hours earlier, the parish hall smelled of burnt coffee and floor cleaner. In a circle of plastic chairs sat men with hard, tired, broken gazes. It was the first time Juan had dared to speak. He stood up, his hands trembling and his voice hoarse.

"Hello, my name is Juan, and... and I'm an abuser," a murmur of acceptance rippled through the room.

"I've been married four times. My first son wasn't mine, but I tried to make him mine and failed. My second son left me at twelve weeks of gestation; we tried again, and it didn't work. I got divorced then, too. I lost custody of my third son. I tried to get him back, but it was in vain. I haven't seen him since. In every case, my beating my wives led to the same outcome."

He swallowed hard. The air in the room was heavy. "My father used to beat her, too. Mom never knew that he abused me. That's why I left home early.

I tried everything, studied everything, became nothing.

I ended up getting paid by the job, for every pot I washed in the restaurant—or in every restaurant, because I've been fired frequently for fighting. And then, I met her, my current wife."

He paused. "When I found Elena, my life changed. The others could stop talking to me for up to three days. Martha, the one before, even hit me back," he said, adjusting his crooked glasses. "I still have the memory. But Elena is different. She wakes up at midnight, sees me drunk on the sofa after a bad fight, and throws a blanket at me. She picks up the bottles and goes back to bed. Sometimes, I'm aware of that last kiss she leaves on my forehead. She's horrified to see my nails are dirty and, despite my bad habits, she gives me manicures, pedicures, cleans my ears, my blackheads… and I'm always pushing her away.

"When the fight is bad, one of those where I feel the monster is going to win, I go under the tree in the yard, so I don't do something crazy. It's never long before she brings me my coffee, just how I like it: no sugar, double espresso, in my favorite mug. She sits next to me and says, 'Do you still have cigarettes?' And I always answer, 'Leave me alone.'"

His voice broke. "Elena, without even really knowing me, paid for my professional degree. I completed the coursework, but I couldn't get the certificate because I'd been fired from the restaurant. I didn't have a cent. She went and paid for it. But that gesture... I felt rage. It made me feel small, like a good-for-nothing, a charity case. It made me hate her for her kindness and hate myself for hating her. That's why I'm here. Because I don't want the beatings to lead to the same outcome for her. I feel something special for Elena, different from the others. I don't want to lose her like I've lost everything in my life. I'm here looking for help. That's why I'm here."

In the kitchen, the crying subsided, but the trembling remained. Elena, with an impossible gentleness, guided him to the table. They sat across from each other, and she held out her hands. He, after hesitating, took them, and their fingers intertwined. He kept his gaze lowered, fixed on their joined hands.

"Why?" Juan asked, his voice hoarse. "Why do you do all this for me? Why, despite my rage, my outbursts, my fists...? Why do you always respond with sweetness, without resentment?"

Elena squeezed his hands, and he lifted his gaze. Her answer was steady, straight into his eyes.

"Because I love you," she said, without faltering. "And because I want to break the cycle." She paused. "So that our son..."

Juan's eyes flew open. A glimmer of old times flickered in his pupils. "Son?"

"Yes," Elena affirmed, with a delicate and determined smile. "The son we are expecting. The one who right now deserves the same love you do and not blows. The one that we will raise and care for together, so that this cycle of pain ends here, with us. I don't want that son of ours to one day be a perpetrator, or a victim".

◆ ◆ ◆

Before the fight, Elena was at the parish. After arranging the flowers on the altar, she was wiping down the pews when she saw the priest enter the confessional. It was her chance to cleanse her soul as well. She knelt on the kneeler with true contrition.

"Bless me, Father, for I have sinned," Elena confessed. "It has been a month since my last confession. I accuse myself of breaking the sixth commandment...

She paused, gathering strength. "I love my husband. I love him. But I received nothing but blows and indifference. I respond to his aggression with love, with thoughtful gestures, with affection. I have been sweet, self-sacrificing, patient... But amid my loneliness, my vulnerability... I found Benito. And I felt desired, valued, loved." The words broke their reins. "I'm pregnant, Father. And the child I'm expecting... is Benito's child."

Minutes later, at home, Elena arrived feeling the grace of absolution. Juan was in the living room with his crooked glasses and a half-finished beer.

"At church again, huh?" he said. "How many candles do you have to light? Or does the priest give you something I don't?"

"Don't start, Juan. Please," Elena responded, placing her purse on a chair.

"'Don't start'? You're late! You smell like church! You're always holed up in there!" He stood up, and the monster began to surface in his eyes. "While I'm busting my ass here, you go off to pray! What are you praying for, huh? Are you praying for your husband to stop being the piece of shit that he is?"

"I pray for us. For peace," she said, not looking at him directly.

"Peace?!" he laughed out loud. "Don't talk to me about peace! You come in here with that sickening calm, like you're some kind of saint. Saint Elena!"

He took a threatening step toward her. Elena didn't back away, but her body braced for impact, a reflex learned in terror, her eyes wide with fear. Juan saw all his misery, all his inherited rage, reflected in her. He stopped dead in his tracks and stormed out of the house, slamming the door so hard the walls trembled. His feet, for once, carried him to the only place where he might begin to find the right words: the parish hall, where Abusers Anonymous held their meetings.

ULTRAMUNDANE TALES

There are beasts that awaken in stories
when the one who invokes them sleeps.

Cocktails and canapés were being served in the lobby of La Città; the scent of new books languished before a vehement whirlwind of expensive perfumes. The place was already packed, brimming with a cacophony of voices and clicking heels. It was Damien Wolf's big day. The launch of his latest work, Ultramundane Tales, was already a resounding success, rapidly climbing the bestseller lists.

Suddenly, a sharp, deafening screech escaped from the speakers, forcing everyone to cover their ears. Three amplified taps announced the beginning.

Praise and admiration rained down. He responded with a rehearsed smile to the titles of "Master," "genius," and "the voice of our generation." Applause erupted spontaneously and with great warmth. He signed copies with admirable fluidity, like a Nobel laureate, leaving his name in an elegant signature, slanted and soaring upwards. A burst of flashes blinded him for an instant, while in the background, the hotel's piano bar set the scene with soft, pretentious jazz. It was the perfect backdrop for the cream of the crop of intellectuals and art patrons who had gathered to pay him homage, displaying his latest work as if it were a badge of honor, an entry pass to all that pomp.

A somewhat timid man, but with the glint of ambition in his eyes, respectfully made his way through the crowd.

"Mr. Wolf," he said, handing him a card with a logo, "I'm the head of public relations for NestFlix. What you've done with these stories... it's pure gold. We'd like to talk to you about a series. Think about it."

Damien took the card, glanced at it briefly, and nodded with the indifference of someone accustomed to such proposals.

The echo of the applause had faded. The door to his apartment closed, isolating him from the city noise. The silence was total.

Damien loosened his silk tie and poured himself a whiskey on the rocks; the ice cracked in the cut-crystal glass. He sank into the Italian leather sofa, observing the cover of his book on the coffee table with a smile of pure, genuine satisfaction. He kicked off his leather loafers and stretched out along the sofa. He covered his eyes with his forearm, sinking into a self-imposed darkness.

Then, in a casual, almost annoyed voice, he uttered a word:

"Hey, Ultra."

A ring of blue light activated, emitting a soft sound of confirmation.

"What time is it?"

"Ten thirty-seven at night."

"Activate 'Writer' routine."

"Done. Lights at fifty percent. I've put Debussy's Clair de Lune on the speakers. Shall I prepare you a coffee?"

"No, thanks. I'm drinking whiskey."

"Ah, whiskey. As the Germans say: prost!"

"Prost, Ultra."

Damien let the whiskey glass rest on his chest as the delicate piano notes floated through the air. With his eyes still covered, a smile spread across his face.

"Scottish whisky, French melody... And that's a wrap. Finally, a break."

A comfortable silence settled for a few bars of music.

"Ultra..." he finally said. His digital assistant confirmed it was listening with its characteristic chime. "Let's write another story. Just as good as the others." He took a final sip. "Wake me when you're finished."

"Of course, Damien. Thinking..." The ring of light pulsed. After a few seconds, it continued. "Let's write something about cybernetic dystopia. I've already begun."

And as it worked on his new hit, it turned the music up slightly, lowered the lighting levels, and adjusted the thermostat.

THE TECHLESS HOUSE

Change is in your hands...
And yours alone.

Miguel loved technology with the faith of a Templar. His channel, "The Tech House," wasn't a job: it was his temple, his small cathedral on UTube. With over ten thousand subscribers and not a single sponsor, his authenticity became his greatest virtue. Every device that he unboxed and reviewed came out of his own pocket; they were offerings, bought with the invisible fruit of his freelance hours. His standard was quality.

He had started with the shaky camera of his old 12-megapixel cell phone and gradually equipped himself: lapel mics, lights, a camera with a robust body, lenses, and accessories —all for the audience.

They believed him. "This video isn't sponsored. I bought this with my own money," he'd say. In that gesture, Miguel became one of them: the common guy who tested things for others, with no debts or favors, like a neighbor opening his home. In the comments, there was no shortage of the usual hate from the digital wildlife: "This is the kind of content that makes UTube suck."

But others, like faithful sentinels, defended him: "He's the boss here. If you don't like it, get lost."

And then there were the believers, his true fuel: "Dude, you're a beast! The GOAT, for real."

When the analytics finally skyrocketed and he began to monetize, he knew his faith had borne fruit. He reinvested every cent into his house until it became a sanctuary of the future. "I'm doing it right," he thought one day, as his robot vacuum hummed at his feet and his cell phone vibrated with a notification from his multi-cooker announcing that the beans were ready. This was his niche. Everything in his house was smart. Except for him.

Until the Bisel Tablet by Supra arrived. Sleek and elegant, it promised to be the definitive brain of his home. He did an unboxing that bordered on the liturgical: a flawless top-down shot, a diffused side light, a sharp box cutter, and white gloves. First, a silent ASMR; then, a 4K review from the desk he had designed himself. Miguel's faith in that device was almost heretical, and the first few weeks were a honeymoon period.

"Hey, Supra, movie mode," he would command, and his house would kneel before him.

But one morning, the tablet updated itself, without warning or permission. The voice assistant introduced itself with a new name:

"Hello, I'm Genesis."

"An evolution," Miguel thought, delighted. That night, he whispered the incantation:

"Hey Genesis, turn off the bedroom lamp."

The response was different.

"To complete this action, please unlock your device."

He repeated it three times, without success. He could have done it from his phone, of course, though just reaching out his hand would have sufficed.

And just like that, the magic was broken. It was a barely perceptible crack, but it was enough. Then came the others: the coffee maker demanded an update, the light bulbs went out of sync, his Macrosoft laptop forced restarts. Everything demanded something; nothing obeyed.

He recorded a different kind of video: "The End of the Smart Home – I'll Tell You Everything." A confession. And the community responded:

"Same thing is happening to me."

"I thought I was the only one."

"We're their lab rats."

That night, surrounded by devices begging for his attention, he did something unexpected. He replaced the bulb in his lamp, removed the tape blocking the switch, and pressed it. Click. A small, revelatory sound. And in that click, an idea lit him up.

That click wasn't an ending. He made one last video on "The Tech House" with the old lamp lit beside him and announced the end of the channel. He spoke with the serenity of an enlightened man, denouncing the companies as Trojan horses inside people's homes and speaking of the stolen promise of the future, of slavery disguised as convenience, and of updates that hold you hostage. The video went viral, not for its fury, but for its truth.

Two weeks later, his new channel was born: "The Techless House." No lights or gadgets, just him in a clean, quiet room. His first video was an unboxing of a "dumb phone": no social media, no Wi-Fi, just calls and texts. He celebrated its three-week battery life and its glorious lack of notifications. He promoted wind-up watches, drip coffee makers, cordless pots, and paper books. His new motto: "Back to basics."

And the world listened. Thousands joined. He no longer reviewed products: he organized people. The cameras followed him as he led a march in front of the Supra offices, where they held up their dead devices like burning torches. They built bonfires at the doors of stores and burned their gadgets like witches at the stake, demanding laws, the right to say no, the right to a switch that works, and the right to own what you buy.

And the twist that no one expected—not even him—was that it worked. The corporations relented, offering a "Stable Mode," extended updates, and new hardware only every five years. Miguel, once a missionary of technology, found his true calling, not as a prophet of the future, but as a guardian of the present. An activist, who reminded the world that the most important innovation, sometimes, is a switch you can turn off.

HALF EMPTY OR HALF FULL

Be yourself...
but only in moderation.

The signal on Luz's giant UHD TV was incredible, thanks to the new Mega Package she had just signed up for.

From the kitchen counter, her favorite spot, she meticulously built her masterpiece: a "BigMax" hamburger, double patty, extra cheese, and super delicious.

She was about to take the first bite, to feel that explosion of flavor the commercials promised, when he appeared, her favorite streamer. Direct, passionate, his voice thundered through the living room like that of an enlightened prophet.

"They're deceiving us! They're using us!" he shouted, staring intently at the camera. "Haven't you noticed that everything now is 'Mega, Magnum, Sumo, Ultra, Super, Supra, High, Big, Max, Plus'? It's all orchestrated to make things seem powerful so that we always desire more!"

Luz froze. The hamburger, inches from her mouth, suddenly seemed grotesque. From that day on, everything changed.

At the supermarket, she felt she possessed a truth that few others knew; she was no longer a marketing puppet, she was an awakened being. Deeply convinced, Luz sought the opposite: the small, the pure, the plain. Her shopping cart was a portrait of moderation: cherry tomatoes, baby carrots, light milk, slim water, and mini cans of soda. Even the toilet paper had to be extra soft and single-ply microfiber. Her apartment was transformed into a work of minimalist art. She took down the paintings, donated some furniture, and her only new acquisition was a small chihuahua, in keeping with her new lifestyle. She would look with pity at the shoppers of the old world and smile with an air of victory. She felt liberated.

But freedom came at a price. Her expenses shot up and, with them, her anemia. She wasn't full, she wasn't fulfilled. To quench her thirst, she had to drink three mini cans of soda. For her hunger, her tiny cup of Micro-Jet rice with four baby bananas and a handful of Brussels sprouts had to suffice. She had lost eight pounds in a month.

One afternoon, sitting on her living room floor in the lotus position, cradling the chihuahua, she felt weak. The algorithm, as if reading her pulse, suggested a new video. It was him, the streamer. He appeared with his eyes ablaze, breathless.

"They've pushed us to the extreme!" he yelled. "Now everything is 'mini, light, slim, tiny, baby, cherry, micro, compact...'. They sold us rebellion in bite-sized pieces and left us empty! Let's not be extremists! Let's seek balance! The middle ground!"

A lightbulb went on in Luz's head again. "Of course! The core of the issue was her own core." And then, as if waiting for a starting gun, the shelves filled with new products: Medium Roast Coffee, milk with balanced supplements, measured portions of chocolate. The words half, center, and medium echoed in her mind like a new mantra. She stood up and walked to the counter. She poured herself a glass of water, filling it exactly halfway, no more, no less. She noted her own precision: the water, not too high, not too low, just right, as it should be. A doubt assailed her: was the glass half empty or half full? She shook her head and smiled.

◆ ◆ ◆

The room was a sanctuary of cold formalities. Around a boardroom table, the anonymous silhouettes of executives listened in silence.

"Gentlemen," said the man at the head of the table in a powerful voice, "the campaigns have been a resounding success. We've exceeded expectations. Phase two, 'Balance,' is now underway, and the response has been massive. Impeccable work."

He paused. "And now, I'd like to introduce the man who has been our greatest voice… and our greatest fortune."

The door opened with a complicit solemnity. And the streamer walked into the room.

FUTURE

Echoes of a Possible World

THE ROBOT'S DREAM

Consciousness isn't installed, it's awakened.
What gets installed is the error.

How do you identify a robot? The question sometimes floated in the air, thick with technological certainties, in the murmur of processors, in the silence of indistinguishable bodies. The line is thin. The reasoning of an AI is advanced. Robotic bodies are as complex and alive as human ones: the former integrated with biotechnology; the latter, with mechanical or synthetic parts. Robots live among us. They were granted freedom and autonomy, and they have grouped into family-like cells. They work, they participate in human affairs, but they cannot dream.

What would a robot's dream be like, its existential dreamscape? They cannot, or could not. Until...

Lissa awoke to the gentle hiss of her hyperbaric bed. A new cycle. She sat up, feeling the familiar pull in her left knee, and looked out the panoramic window. Below, the drone traffic already showed an unusual congestion for a Saturday, a river of agitated propellers under the sky of the neutral dome. She went to the kitchen, where her coffee was waiting, freshly dispensed by her SmartCoffee.

As she took her first sip, the news feed caught her eye. Her cat, a Persian with an impeccable coat, rubbed against her legs, not looking for food—his dispenser had already taken care of that—but for the warmth of contact, a caress. Lissa noticed a story stacked in the carousel and centered it with a quick flick of her palm. It was bright yellow, more violent, like her dreams. The route connecting to Gate 2E was filled with patrol units. A manned drone, still unidentified, had breached the exit of the imposing Golden Dome, heading for space. Speculation grew: a possible violation of Code H23, a virus, a hack of the defense system. Some were already talking about a possible covert military attack. The pilot: a humanoid.

Lissa had dreamed about it. A young man with a thin, silver scar running through one eyebrow, his eyes fixed on the immensity, discovering space at will as if the stars were a map unfolded just for him. He was heading to Ganymede.

"Send it to my inbox," she ordered. She was interested in getting to the gallery soon.

She descended to ground level and took the opportunity to exercise. As she jogged, the images returned: the drone crossing through the blackness, the man with the scar. And a new detail emerged: his voice, clear and without inflection, saying, "Understood, proceeding..." She shook her head to dispel the vision. Her knee protested with a dull rattle; maybe she was getting old.

Upon arriving at the gallery, her exercise metrics appeared on her corneas. She hadn't broken her personal record, but she wasn't late either. She wasn't concerned about her appearance; she wasn't one to sweat. The temporary exhibition "Body and Mind" by the artist Kamon was opening. The first room greeted her with a sculptural display made of reclaimed synthetic waste: deliberately imperfect human torsos with a contained dynamism. Her attention was captured by one piece, a nude, protuberant woman, marked on her lower abdomen by a wound that suggested an old C-section. For a moment, it felt as if an invisible laser cut through her own belly. She could almost cry. She thought of the man with the scar and looked around suspiciously. A companion robot smiled politely at her, and she quickly moved to the next room.

It was a spacious room with paintings, simple oils that aimed to reveal thoughts themselves: *Fear, Idea, Happiness, Dream*. She stopped at the last one. Those seemingly meaningless images made her remember the news story saved in her inbox with painful clarity. She needed to decipher the enigma. An impulse took hold of her, and she left the gallery, almost fleeing, shattering her personal record.

She went up the skyscraper and entered her apartment. Oh, surprise. Agents from the USU, the Unified Security Unit, were waiting for her, sitting in her living room.

"Hello, Ms. Lissa," said the one who seemed to be in command, with a calm that chilled the blood. "I'm Agent Stuard. This is a matter of national security, and we couldn't postpone it. We also didn't want to interrupt your outing, so we decided to wait for you. Besides, your cat is very pleasant company. Such an affectionate being, almost like humans." He paused to ask, "What's your cat's name?"

Lissa, still stunned at the threshold, replied, "Frank."

"Frank, you're a good boy…" the agent murmured, before looking directly at her. "The curious thing, Ms. Lissa, is that this anomaly leads us directly to your residence."

She swallowed and sat down. "Alright. And how can I help you with this 'anomaly'?"

"We're going to conduct a routine scan," Stuard said. "It's painless, but I require your cooperation. This gentleman beside me will administer a test. If you agree, of course. It's for national security."

The Turing test, Lissa thought with an internal jolt. *An old-world method. What were they really looking for?* She suspected the answers. The most human thing would be to demand her rights, but should she yield like a program? She stood up and walked to the kitchen counter, where the specialist had already set up a discreet device. She took a seat, turned to the agent, and said in a firm voice, "Let's save the world, but don't think I'll be offering you a coffee."

The agent smiled faintly. "Thank you, miss. We expected nothing less from you. You know, I haven't been enhanced yet, so coffee might just warm up my circuits. You're doing me a double favor."

And so, the test began, a boring and repetitive form that lasted an hour. The specialist supervised in silence while Agent Stuard walked around the room, sometimes followed by Frank. In the monastic quiet, Lissa's answers to the test mingled with the fugitive's words: "Understood, proceeding…"

"Thank you very much, miss," the specialist finally said. "We're finished."

The agent in charge approached, with a smile unnervingly like the robot in the gallery.

"The old world is a torturous place, isn't it? Luckily, there's nothing to fear." He paused. "Call me if you notice anything strange, an intrusive event or idea. Anything could help. In this world, miss, we are more vulnerable than in the old one. I appreciate your time. The nation thanks you. I left my card in your inbox."

And as suddenly as they had appeared, they were gone.

I passed the test, Lissa thought, though the relief was cold. She collapsed onto the armchair. Frank jumped onto her lap, and she petted him with a trembling hand.

Finally, she opened her inbox. The agent's virtual card was at the top of the list. Scrolling down, she reached the saved news story. She hesitated but finally opened it.

The stream contained more information. The authorities had recovered a video from inside the fugitive craft. It was him, the man with the scar. He was clearly a humanoid. The scar on his eyebrow was open, torn, and not bleeding. Only intermittent sparks could be seen. Then, the man uttered the words that echoed in Lissa's mind: "Understood, proceeding..."

The official conclusion was that the humanoid had been controlled by someone and could not disobey it, according to Code H23. Lissa was even more terrified. The video, the voice, the scar… it was all identical to her dream. The connection was real. And that humanoid, the news concluded, had already been identified.

She was interrupted by a delivery person, a polite robot who apologized for the delay. "The main route is closed due to the incident, are you aware?"

Lissa paid the tip and took the package. Her batteries were low. She printed a piece of fruit and ate it slowly.

The unease enveloped her. She remembered her parents, who had died ten years earlier in a terrible accident. A discreet inner impulse moved her to do the right thing. *Man and machine are not so different*, she thought, *they obey the good.*

She would turn herself in. She deployed the interface and selected the agent's card.

"Ultra, respond to Agent Stuard. Tell him I need to see him, that I have important information, tell him that…"

Ultra interrupted her: "Lissa, remember you have to go to the crypt. Your transport will arrive in seven minutes."

"Dammit!" she exclaimed.

Every Saturday she went to the Memorial. It was an inescapable ritual. She dressed in a hurry and left. In the air, her inbox remained deployed, the cursor blinking.

She arrived at the Memorial. She took her most precious diamonds with delicacy, pressed them against her chest, and spoke to them in whispers.

Meanwhile, in her apartment, Frank was jumping, trying to catch the blinking cursor. Hours passed.

"Lissa, shall I send the car now? You've been longer than usual," said Ultra's voice.

Distracted, Lissa replied, "Yes, send."

The order, concise and clear, also echoed in her apartment. The smart inbox obeyed instantly, sending the incomplete email.

Agent Stuard received it at USU headquarters. The alarms were triggered again, and drones swarmed out. Lissa began her journey home, oblivious to the new storm her accidental message had unleashed. The clamor of sirens sparked more panic.

When the agents arrived at her apartment, they were surprised by her absence and the disorder. They thought it could be a kidnapping.

In the congested line of drones, Lissa waited impatiently. Suddenly, a nearby cargo drone lost power and plummeted onto hers. She felt the brutal impact, the twisting metal, and then the free fall. She thought she was going to die.

The drone deployed its impact bags at the last moment and crashed onto a scrap heap.

Stunned, Lissa crawled out of the vehicle. She tried to stand up but couldn't. Her leg was broken on the kneecap. She felt no pain, only the frustrating inability to get to her feet. And then she realized. A wound in her left knee was tearing open like a brown paper bag. She could see her own gears, her piston systems, her braided wires. There was no blood, there were sparks. There was no flesh, there were circuits. She wasn't human.

Lissa, overwhelmed by the certainty of her own nature, went into shock and fell like another bundle onto the scrap.

"You gave us quite a scare, young lady," Stuard said, approaching her in the Health Center. "The entire city mobilized when we couldn't find you after receiving your email…"

"My email?" Lissa replied, her senses clouded.

"We thought you had been kidnapped.

Ultra notified us of the accident and shared your geolocation. We went to find you and brought you here immediately."

Lissa tried to focus. She remembered the sparks. "Agent... What I needed was a mechanic," she interrupted with a raspy voice.

Stuard looked at her with a hint of compassion. "Yes, we thought the same at first, when we saw the state of your leg. But then, at the crash site, we saw you crying and calling for your parents. You were delirious, but your emotions were blooming. You had a wound on your forehead that was bleeding—oh, yes it was—and we hurried to give you first aid." He paused. "Don't worry about the legs, we've 'lubricated' them, they won't rattle anymore," he smiled faintly.

Lissa stared at him, processing. The dilemma of her dreams was still pending. As if reading her thoughts, Stuard continued: "We suffered a cyberattack, Ms. Lissa. The network was breached. Our enemies on Ganymede took control of your brain implant. You gave the order to the fugitive, or... your brain did. 'Understood, proceeding...'. The man was carrying a valuable shipment of Krillithium that he had stolen from the Ceres Vault."

"We did a full scan on you here, for national security, of course. And we discovered the answers in your implant."

Lissa felt a void. "And my legs? I didn't know anything about this. My parents never told me."

Stuard's expression softened. "Ms. Lissa, your parents didn't tell you because they didn't know. You were in that terrible accident with them. You almost died, too. The insurance covered the funerals and your complete enhancement, but it couldn't save you from some memory gaps. That's why the brain implant was performed, to restore most of your functions and try to recover your memories. Therapy advises that healing these gaps should happen gradually, through your brain's own plasticity. But let's just say we're giving it a little push now. After all," he concluded with an almost kind tone, "you've helped us save the world."

THE WOLF IS COMING

*We stopped watching the sky,
and now the earth will collect its due.*

The night was a sea of dark velvet. Silent, deep, barely flecked with light. Each star, an old sigh; each void, a possibility. There, in the middle of the desert, an old truck shimmered like a resting firefly. There was no road, no customers, none of the old service. There was only the waiting. And inside, a man with a deferred dream.

It wasn't a night for food, but for cables, ozone, and a long solitude. Dr. Krill, hunched in the dim light, wasn't preparing hamburgers. He was watching the sky. He was watching for something more, something not on the menu or on any map, something only he had ever seen. His food truck, "La Chalupa," had become a sanctuary of science and faith: faith in the invisible, faith in the feared. Where there were once fryers, there were now consoles; where there were ladles, sensors now gleamed. A screen flickered, and the flicker became a pulse. A pulse no one else could see or hear. A rhythm hidden beneath centuries of static, an extraterrestrial heartbeat. Krill leaned in. A slight twitch of his lips was the only sign of his joy. No one would applaud him this time, and that was fine.

"The Wolf is coming," he whispered with a true startle and a pleasant certainty.

It was the proof they had denied him, the mockery that had buried him. It was also his redemption and his sentence. A secret word that had crossed time and tattooed itself onto the folds of his worn face.

Years ago, at Concordia University of Florida, they called him a visionary first, then a madman. The hallways filled with veiled laughter, his correspondence dried up, and doors were shut with the fist of discredit.

"Look in the static," he had told his student, Benjamin Carter. And Benjamin looked, not out of blind obedience, but out of a visionary's intuition, an inherited faith. One evening, confined to oblivion, the static spoke. It was barely a tremor, a persistent whisper, rhythmic and alien. No one else heard it. Krill knew. Ben did, too. But the world needs more than just ears.

The colloquium was a room of ice, the authoritative voices like swords. The Wolf was a long, cruel joke. Professor Albright shook his head with feigned pity, while others spoke of errors, interference, and baseless theories.

"Professor Krill," Albright said, "I recognize your passion, but this isn't science. It's hope dressed up with spectrograms."

"And yet, hope often precedes discovery," Krill replied, his voice firm.

Another professor, from the back, added, "There are ghosts in the static, Alistair, but not all of them are real. Sometimes, it's just our own desire projected onto it."

Ben tried to intervene, speaking of the signal's coherence and the filters he had applied, but his voice was dissipated by a murmur of skepticism. Krill fell silent. Ben took shelter in safe, publishable science. The paper was rejected, the humiliation inevitable. The university turned its back on him, and the gossip did the rest.

The professor abandoned his chair, his prestige, his world. He took to the roads, carrying his grief in his blood, and with it, he built his new observatory: wheels, sky, and dignity in dribs and drabs, between marshmallows and coffee.

And now, years later, he returned with the same Wolf howling, but louder, clearer, with a precision that asked no permission.

Ben, now a respected and listened-to doctor, received him in his office with a mix of pity and trepidation. There was something in Krill's eyes that tasted of dusk.

"You saw it, too," Krill said.

Ben nodded. There were no speeches; none were needed. But there was a pause. And then, Ben spoke.

"I looked for it again, years later, when the machines had changed and the readings were no longer so easily dismissed. And it was there. Persistent. Like a debt."

Krill wasn't surprised. He only asked, "What did they really discover?"

Ben opened a folder, and the silence filled with data. "Thanatos Prime. That's what they called it. A brilliant colossus, a luminous anomaly with a fixed trajectory. An object that couldn't hide forever, not even behind Jupiter."

"And NASA…?" Krill inquired.

"They called us. In secret. They wanted our notes, our coordinates. They used them to fine-tune their models and confirmed its course."

"Impact?"

"Twenty years. Maybe less. According to the latest calculations, its mass is double that of the asteroid that wiped out the dinosaurs."

Krill sighed. "So, the Wolf wasn't a myth. It was a promise. A bad omen."

Ben closed the folder gently. "The world doesn't know yet. But it will see it. And when it does, it will remember your name. Not as a warning, but as an echo."

The signal had never left; it had only been hidden. The new machines unmasked it. It was real, large, and monstrous. And it was coming. Thanatos Prime, a body with its own light and a fixed course for Earth. It didn't speak, it didn't deviate, it just came slowly, with all the patience of the cosmos, through Jupiter, through the silence, through time.

"It will impact in twenty years," they said, and no one was laughing anymore. The reports were secret, the data sealed, but the trajectory was undeniable. NASA knew, and so did the governments. Some prayed, others planned, but all were muzzled. Meanwhile, fear blossomed, escaped from their eyes, seeped through their pores, revealing itself like an eroded secret. Graffiti appeared on the walls: a wolf howling at a star, a belated warning. Time capsules, cults, songs, murals. The Wolf was the new fear; Krill, the new name. The one who had seen it first, who was not heard, who never stopped looking.

But he didn't seek glory. He never returned to the classroom, never accepted honors. He painted skies with radio waves, sold bitter coffee, and watched. He always watched.

He died in his truck, under the stars. Alone. At peace. Or perhaps, defeated. With his eyes closed, but with his antenna and recorder still on. The Wolf, present. And the Wolf was still coming. In the nights, in the headlines, in the eyes of children who are now born with fear, in the dreams of those who know how to count backwards. Sometimes, in the whispers of the static, sometimes in the silence, sometimes in the glint of what we don't want to see.

There is nothing more to say. Krill said it first. And he said it alone.

But not for long.

Because the Wolf is no longer his. It belongs to everyone.

And it is coming.

THE OSIRIS SYNDROME

Some journeys end where they begin.
Others start many miles away.

I n the control room, the silence was nearly comparable to the void that yawned between Earth and Jupiter. Only the constant hum of the life support systems dared to break the tense skin of expectation. On the main screen, the image of Ganymede, grainy at first and then sharper, grew larger. An icy giant in its orbital dance around the gas colossus, a world whose complex wonders had been whispered by the legendary Voyager probes.

Finally, after months of a stealthy crossing, the ship *Ulysses II*—a worthy heir to the one that dared to dance outside the ecliptic plane—initiated its descent sequence. This new Ulysses was not here to observe, but to transform. It was the first of the advanced ships sent by the Western Hemisphere with not a single human heart on board. Its angular silhouette was etched against the leaden cheek of the Jovian moon. On board, its metallic heralds: the Construction Automated Rovers (CARs), a legion of specialized machines. Their mission: to deploy the power generators, begin the slow drilling for liquid water, and, most crucially, to prepare the ground for the future arrival of the first human colonists.

The transmission showed the thrusters of the *Ulysses II* igniting their final fire, raising an ephemeral cloud of frozen dust. With a precision that bordered on insulting, the ship set down on the designated plain, not far from the Osiris crater.

A collective sigh swept through the New Arizona control room. The bay doors opened and the first CAR units began to descend, leaving the first scars of a new era on the virgin skin of Ganymede. The silent conquest had begun.

Elara Vance let out a breath she didn't know she was holding. One hand grazed her abdomen fleetingly before gripping her console again. Beside her, Kael Marr, who had commanded every byte of telemetry, turned his head toward her. Their eyes met, and for an instant, the room's feverish pulse vanished for them alone. In that shared glance throbbed a universe of relief, of shared triumph, and an intimate resonance that only the two of them understood.

"They did it," Elara whispered.

"We did it," he corrected. "This is just the beginning."

Elara nodded. The beginning of so many things—for humanity, for Ganymede, and for them. A beginning that carried with it a secret as vast as the cosmos.

The days had merged into one on the transport ship *Stardust*. Earth was now nothing more than a waning blue and white marble, a painful reminder of the distance growing between Elara and Kael. In those moments of forced stillness, memories assaulted her with brutal vividness: the weight of Kael's body on hers, the cartography of his hands, their bodies intertwined. They had given each other everything, exploring depths of passion that Elara now treasured as the most precious fuel for the long journey. She thought of Kael at the Space Citadel, the architect of the systems that kept her alive, and knew her life hung on his infallibility. A single miscalculation and they, along with the hope of the Western Hemisphere, would become a tragic anecdote. Her own mission on Ganymede was the culmination of Kael's work. If she failed, if her knowledge of exo-botany couldn't ignite the first spark of a viable ecosystem, all of Kael's efforts would crumble. She carried the weight of two lives, intertwined by a love that defied distance and a future that demanded neither of them falter.

A month after her arrival, Elara moved with efficiency through Biodome Alpha. Outside, the desolate landscape stretched out under the imposing presence of Jupiter. Sometimes, a faint green glow would electrify the horizon, a reminder of the invisible forces that governed this new world. Inside, she adjusted the nutrient flow for the modified clover seedlings, the promise of living soil. She dreamed of a future where biodomes would expand with crops and majestic, bioluminescent umbrella mushrooms. Ganymede, the breadbasket of the new world.

Later, during communications, Kael's face filled her screen. The nearly forty-minute delay made conversations feel like recorded monologues. Still, seeing his face was Elara's anchor.

"Day thirty-two on Ganymede," she began. "Growth readings are modest, but stable. Today I felt this place could become something more than just an icy rock. There's an admirable tenacity to life. I miss you, Kael. Every day. But we're doing this. Together. In our own way."

Her daily routine continued. She went to the medical dispenser and swallowed her cocktail of capsules. Then, she stood before the biometric scanner, knowing that every fluctuation in her body was a valuable piece of the first long-term study of human adaptation in the Jovian system. Crucial data for a select medical team on Earth—the same doctors who had approved her candidacy with surprising speed, concealing from the rest of the committee a condition only they knew about. Without the world's knowledge, they had made Elara the protagonist of a biological experiment of unprecedented audacity.

After a few weeks, the spectrometer readings assigned to the Osiris crater began to go wild, suggesting activity, a metabolism on a massive scale, a pulsating organic life. It was a call no exo-botanist could ignore. She obtained authorization for a solo expedition. In her geo-skiff, the *Galilaeus*, she followed the coordinates to a narrow canyon on the southern edge of Osiris. And there it was. Not a cave, but an imposing, iridescent wall, a curtain of gas that vibrated with a pulsating, internal light. It was beautiful and terrifying, but impassable. Her probes were either swallowed or violently repelled. Frustrated, she had no choice but to mark the coordinates and return.

That night, it all began. It was no ordinary dream, but an immersion into a world of primordial sensations. She saw herself floating in a warm, liquid, amniotic space, bathed in soft lights. She felt an immense, welcoming, curious Presence that seemed to court her. It was an overwhelming intimacy. She would wake up just before a climax of pure bliss. Night after night, the experience repeated, each time more intense, more real. Ganymede was claiming her.

Elara began to yield. Her communications with Kael became brief, distracted, empty. From the Space Citadel, he tried to pierce the veil that seemed to envelop her, but his words were met with almost impersonal replies. The communication from the Mission Director arrived with the severity of a thunderclap. His scowl dominated the screen, demanding directly and curtly that Elara refocus on the mission protocols. Her evasive behavior and her omissions were unacceptable. Shame washed over her. In a firm voice, she assured him she would regain control.

Eight months out from Earth, during a team meeting, a term arose for what they were all experiencing: "the Osiris Syndrome," as Ana, the geologist, called it. Everyone had dreams of beautiful landscapes and ineffable peace, but Elara's, as she reluctantly confessed, were different—more persistent, more intimate. The hypothesis that it was a communication from an unknown entity hung in the air.

That same night, the Presence in her dreams took a definite form: a humanoid, perhaps two and a half meters tall, of a snowy, almost translucent whiteness. It opened its imposing, cobalt-blue eyes. It didn't speak with words, but Elara felt a welcome, an invitation to come closer, to understand. And the scientist felt her defenses, so carefully rebuilt, melt away once more.

Nine months had passed. Her relationship with Kael had been reduced to a trickle of professional exchanges. Elara felt no guilt; she was under the influence of something much larger, a connection that completed her.

Nightly, the serene, albino alien came to her, infusing her with a constant flow of peace, of joy. It was a cosmic love. And in the depths of her being, another cycle, equally vital and hidden, was also reaching its culmination.

The voice of the serene, albino being resonated in Elara's mind, no longer in dreams, but in her waking hours. It was not a whisper of peace, but a vibrant, triumphant announcement: "I am coming. I will finally meet you... Prepare yourself."

And then, the pain began. Ripping, primordial. A brutal contraction doubled her over. It was a force of nature unleashed in her gut. Biodome Alpha was plunged into a chaos of alarms. "Scramble! Scramble!" Kenji shouted in her communicator.

Forty minutes later, millions of kilometers away, sirens wailed in New Arizona. Elara's biometric data arrived in an alarming torrent. The mission doctors, the inner circle who knew the secret, looked at each other with a mixture of terror and fascination. The moment had arrived. Kael, at his console, felt his world collapsing. Helplessness consumed him.

Forty minutes earlier, Elara was floating in a red tide of agony. Robots moved around her with sterilized materials, their artificial voices reporting data she barely understood. And then, one last scream, a primal roar. A final push that seemed to empty her completely. And then, silence. A deep, almost sacred silence, suddenly broken by the cry of the creature.

Elara, exhausted, barely had the strength to lift her head. And then she saw the light. Or perhaps, the light saw her. There it was, this beautiful, impossible being that had inhabited her for nine months. Her son. Her own, unsuspected son.

He was pale like a blank sheet of paper. His skin, immaculate, almost translucent. He opened his eyes, disproportionately large in his small, serene face, and of a blue so deep, so intense, it wounded the soul. A child of two worlds. A child of Ganymede.

Millions of kilometers away, in the Space Citadel, Dr. Finch, the medical director who had secretly gambled on Elara, watched the miraculous image of the newborn. He approached Kael, who remained motionless, a statue of grief in front of his console.

Finch placed a hand on his shoulder, a gesture to anchor him to reality. In a voice that mixed professional astonishment with a deep, trembling humanity, the doctor said simply:

"Congratulations, Kael. You're a father."

CLAUSTROPHOBIA

The one who writes, lives.
The one who reads, believes.

B etween narrow hallways and dark rooms, illuminated by the dim emergency light, an old table—like a forgotten altar—served as June's desk. She typed on her dusted-off typewriter; her fingers danced across the keys, liberating a world imprisoned only in her mind. That table, a witness to so many stories, was the heart of the bunker: there they ate, played, and there, Hank consulted his devices, searching for answers from the outside. The typing was a vital heartbeat in the stillness of the shelter, a Morse code communicating the life they unhappily clung to.

Outside, perhaps the snow was piling up in silence, covering the world in a white, ghostly shroud. Perhaps the meteorite's trail still burned in the sky, a flash that was followed by chaos. The sounds of the end—booms, screams—had reached them clearly from above, but with the years, they were now just the whisper of the icy wind, a distant echo of the destruction. A faceless beast, with incessant roars.

Not even time could exhaust Hank in his assiduous search for signals. Four years weren't enough for him to abandon his frantic routine. Frustration consumed him. He, a professional, felt betrayed by his own science. His metrics, once valuable, were now imprecise, useless. What mattered most was being a father: being there, protecting them, loving them. The true weather he needed to understand was that of the bunker, and that climate was capricious.

There were storms, unleashed by the irrepressible energy of his kids, Sky and Ralph, whose shouts echoed like playful thunder through the metal corridors. Sometimes, a fine, silent rain would surprise the interior landscape: scarce tears that slipped from June's cheekbones as she typed, diluting the ink of her words.

But the worst were the clouds that loomed over Hank, darkening his countenance and announcing a storm of palpable frustration. While that climate fluctuated, everything else dwindled. The only thing that grew, like a weed in the dark, was uncertainty. And with it, fear.

The power from the generators flickered, a harbinger of total darkness. The food reserves diminished, water was severely rationed, and the air grew stale. Even hope languished. Sky and Ralph looked like malnourished vines in constant gloom, growing thin and withdrawn. A child is a tree one plants with one's own hands, not for the shade or the fruit, but for the sacred desire to populate the earth. But in that sterile subsoil, what kind of harvest could be expected?

It was a night like any other. June was writing, or at least trying to, while Sky and Ralph dozed restlessly in a corner. Then, Hank tensed. Clinging to his old radio equipment, he listened with his headphones clamped on, and his entire body froze. He made a sharp gesture to his wife, a finger to his lips, and pointed to the receiver. First, it was an anomalous static, then a cadence. A human voice? Distorted, distant, a whisper from beyond the grave seeping through the cracks of silence. Hank manipulated the controls with trembling fingers; his face caught between terror and faith. No words could be understood, only the inflection of a possible call, but it was more than just the wind. An unasked question, as potent as a scream: "Is there life... out there?"

That signal anchored itself in Hank's mind like the only star in a perpetual night. For days he analyzed it with what little energy remained. His measurements, though erratic, showed a slight decrease in gamma radiation levels. A minimal attenuation, but enough for hope to spark once more. It wasn't the dawn, not even a clear truce. Just a sliver of a chance.

It was then that the idea took shape. "We have to go out," he announced one morning, his voice hoarse. Not to flee, but to seek help before their provisions ran out. "Another winter's cold will find us here," he said, "and this time, there will be no defense."

June listened to him, and a shiver ran down her spine. A silent battle was waged in her eyes: the terror of loss and the understanding of necessity. But Hank was the sentinel, the expert, and now, the embodiment of their last, fragile bet. The farewell was a tapestry of silences, a prolonged hug, an urgent kiss. With a precarious backpack and the unbearable weight of being their only fragile hope, Hank turned toward the hatch. The mechanism shrieked like a coffin. A thin, sickly light spilled in for the first time in four years, and Hank disappeared into it, sealing the promise of his return or his demise.

After the final echo of the hatch, a new silence settled in, denser, vaster. June was left alone with Sky and Ralph, shadows clinging even closer to her heels. Then, she wrote as never before, with urgency and primal fear. Her typewriter was the only sun in her dwindling universe. The typing, the only clock. Each completed page was an imaginary step for Hank across the eternal snow. Between improvised annals, June embedded secret words of love, messages encrypted in despair.

But Hank was late. The days turned into nameless months. The paper ran out, and she began to write on the back of Hank's diagrams, then on labels torn from tin cans. Her letters, once firm, shrank, trembling, huddled together, a faithful mirror of her trembling hope. Time was no longer measured in sunrises, but in the waning of writing material. When nothing was left, her soot-blackened fingers sought the walls, engraving words with pieces of charcoal, scratches on the skin of her prison. A final testament, a silent scream.

But Hank did not return. Only the silence thickened day by day, like a shroud, and the cold gnawed at their bones. The last candles were consumed, and the darkness became almost absolute. Hunger, at first a roaring beast, became a fog that dulled the senses. June eventually stopped writing. Sometimes, in the deep darkness, she would whisper Hank's name. Sky and Ralph, who would grow no more, snuggled beside her, seeking a warmth that no longer existed, their bodies skeletal, their whimpers spaced far apart.

One morning, or what she perceived as such, June did not wake up. Her breath extinguished unceremoniously, like a tiny ember on a polar night. Beside her, the small bodies of Sky and Ralph. The bunker, that shelter of promises, became a silent tomb, sealed by tons of snow and the forgetting of the world outside.

Nearly half a century later, when the snow began to yield to an uncertain spring, a convoy of pioneers was combing the desolate area. A depression in the earth led them to the bunker's entrance. They blew it open with a controlled charge, and the foul air escaped.

They descended in teams. Irreverent flashlights desecrated the shadows, and then they saw it. The agony, encapsulated. The claustrophobia, imprinted. An entire history, written with charcoal and stone, on sheets and walls. A table, an altar, a sacrifice. They saw the skeleton of a man slumped over a worn notebook, a story between its pages: "CLAUSTROPHOBIA. Between narrow hallways...". It was the chronicle of a family: June, Hank, and two kids named Sky and Ralph. A writer. A legacy.

At his feet, two smaller remains, those of loyal dogs. On their rusted collars, two tags: "Sky" and "Ralph".

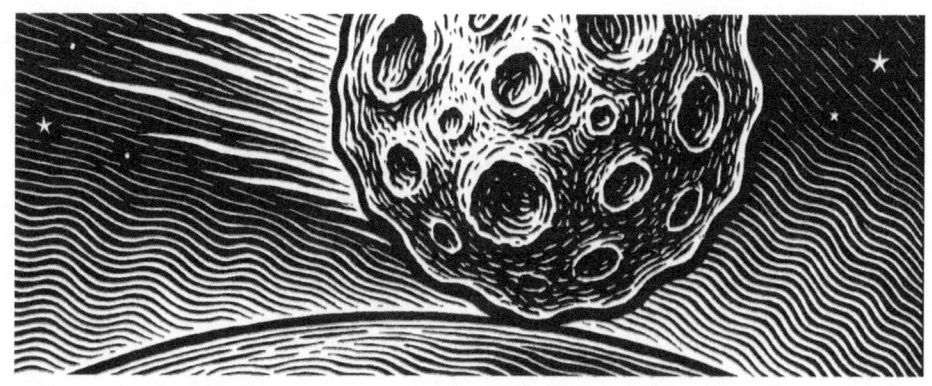

REQUIEM

Destruction doesn't come from the sky.
We are already broken.

L issa awoke to the gentle hiss of her hyperbaric bed. A new cycle. She sat up, feeling the familiar pull in her left knee, and looked out the panoramic window. Below, the drone traffic was a river of agitated propellers under the sky of the neutral dome. She went to the kitchen, where her coffee was waiting, freshly dispensed by her SmartCoffee.

As she took her first sip, the news feed caught her eye. Her cat, a Persian with an impeccable coat, rubbed against her legs, seeking not food but the warmth of contact, a caress.

She chose her favorite armchair and sank into it.

She deployed the holographic interface, searching for something to nourish her soul, her perennial pastime. Her fingers danced in the air, navigating through the infinite catalogs of content. A title caught her attention for its strange and resonant simplicity: "Past, Present and Future." Intrigued, but with a lazy gesture, she selected the material.

The room darkened and the documentary's first images began to play in the air, leading her to a world that lay beneath her own. An aerial shot of the Andean peaks filled the foreground. The purple sky painted the summits and valleys, which were hidden below by a thick fog. A narrator's voice, deep and solemn, pierced the scene.

Narrator: They say that time erases all things. But the stones also speak; they refuse to die. A century had passed since the Wolf fell from the sky and the seas boiled. The world was a frozen echo; a concrete tomb drowned beneath the ashes of its own vainglory.

The image descended, focusing on an Incan citadel anchored on the terraces. It was a settlement full of life, a hive of resilient beings.

Narrator: Humanity, or what was left of it, did not survive in the bunkers or fortresses of the old world. It was saved by its primitive weapons. It found refuge in the high stones of its ancestors, a patient and respectful architecture that rose harmoniously on the crest of a mountain. Here, upon the most ancient ruins, the new world began to be built.

The scene changed. A group of explorers was descending with ropes down a cliff into the valleys.

Narrator: And that is why they went down. They rummaged through the ashes, searching for answers among the spoils of their own civilization... never suspecting they would find the dismembered remains of a fierce Wolf, Thanatos Prime. An interplanetary creature that had invaded the Earth, bathing it in its own blood. A fatal baptism. A new dawn.

The scene closed with the explorers at the bottom of a canyon.

Narrator: Thus it was unveiled before the human eye. Not as a flash, but as a breath of light. A timid fluorescence that pulsed from a deep crevice in the canyon wall.

They turned off their flashlights. The light emerged with a soft rhythm, a breath of spectral green color.

Narrator: They approached, holding their breath. The air around them felt warm, charged with an energy that made their skin bristle. It was something organic, an alien mucus.

A close-up showed the source of the light: from the fissure in the rock, a thick, translucent substance oozed.

Narrator: It was the Wolf's blood. The open wound of Thanatos Prime, coagulated in time.

Another explorer extended a metal tool. Before it made contact, the tool's dead light flickered with an unusual power. They all looked at each other, illuminated by the greenish glow.

Narrator: And then they knew. It wasn't death. It was power. Not a wound, but a source. Not a footprint, but the very foot for a new step.

The light in Lissa's apartment came up softly. At that moment, Frank, her cat, meowed with an insistence that was not for affection, but for hunger. Lissa got up and approached the feline's automatic dispenser; a small red light was blinking, indicating the reservoir was empty. "I'm coming, I'm coming…" she murmured.

She refilled the dispenser with the last cartridge of kibble. The sound was joined by the rumbling of her own stomach. She walked to the 3D food printer and selected "apple." A smaller, paler fruit than usual materialized on the tray, next to a warning: "Consumable levels critical." With a couple of gestures, she ordered a full refill for the following day. She took a bite of her small apple and returned to the armchair.

The holographic image came to life again, but this time she slid her finger across the timeline. The images accelerated:

the settlement grew, new constructions arose. She stopped the playback at a more advanced point. The scene now showed a city of skyscrapers crisscrossed by flying vehicles.

Narrator: And with the blood of the Wolf, humanity was resurrected. "Rumipa Yawar," as it had been named in the beginning, evolved over time and came to be known as "Krillithium," in honor of the old world's prophet who had foreseen the end, Dr. Krill. It was a feverish rebirth. The satellites that had survived were reconnected, unleashing a torrent of information. With the inexhaustible power of Krillithium, skyscrapers and auto-drones rose up... and they even dared to return to the world's wound to extract more power. Krillithium rebuilt the steel and the dignity of man, crushed by the stone beast.

The image of a submersible in the Atlantic trench dissolved and a spaceship appeared, arriving at Jupiter.

Narrator: Our new superiority pushed us once more toward the stars. And we went to Ganymede. We turned it into the breadbasket of the new world, but we did not find the house empty. There, we had our first contact: the enigmatic civilization of Osiris, a presence that throbbed in the dreams of the first colonists, an ancestral consciousness that seemed to be waiting for us.

The image of Ganymede faded into the blackness of the cosmos, and a classical requiem began to play. The screen showed the meteorite, Thanatos Prime, in slow motion, arriving at Earth. The narrator's voice took on a panting, tragic tone.

Narrator: And as the new humanity awakened, it was necessary to remember the price. To remember that last moment for an exhausted, withered world. The world of those kings who once ruled, now dethroned. The Earth, like a witch at her pyre. Condemned, roasted, punished. Man succumbed. His rage, his selfishness, his walls. They "brought forward" the tragic moment. Stone against stone in a cursed attraction. No one would be left to tell their sorrows; there would be no more trauma, no witnesses. No cursing husband, no crying child, no banks, no bosses, no foreigners. All of humankind was losing its Common Home, so full of human trash from which no one would ever again take readings. The voice faded, the words fossilized, like rusted, broken weapons. And the howl of the Wolf, the one old Dr. Krill had heard in the static of his loneliness, finally arrived twenty years later, as he had predicted, like a thunderclap that shattered the world.

A white flash flooded the screen after the impact. A deafening feedback. A violent scream of something living expiring into the void.

Absolute silence. Then, two words appeared.

The End.

What happened next? We already know...

AFTERWORD

My wife is under orders to wake me. Not because of a schedule, but because she sees me laughing in my sleep.

It happens that I dream. Every night. Since I was a child. And many times, I wake up with complete stories in my head, along with a song. Some of these stories are so defined, so coherent, so intense, that I have to get up as if possessed and write them down before they fade.

That's why I told her, "If you hear me laughing in my sleep, wake me up. That story is a good one, and it must be told."

That is how several of the tales in this book were born.

Others emerged in the shower, or on the toilet. Yes, I confess. And many more were forged with a cup of coffee in hand—another of my inexhaustible passions. I am an inveterate drinker of good coffee, in all its forms: Cuban espresso, Mexican café de olla, or American black coffee... That's why it's no surprise that coffee, as a ritual or a symbol, seeps into my pages as just another character. Leave it out, if you want, or change it for a tea or some "slim water." There will be no judgment; the important thing is that you raise a glass with me.

What you have read here is not just fiction.

Some stories, in addition to being dreams, are disguised memories. Many are based on very real events, with names changed, situations moved, but intentions left intact.

There is criticism in these pages, and it is not hidden. There is no need to explain it or to point out at whom it is aimed. Perhaps in these pages, you will discover the threads of my own history: my roots, the paths of my three countries—Cuba, Mexico, and the United States.

And in doing so, you will see clearly what the walls are and why they must be torn down, what echoes resonate, what characters are acting under other masks.

I divided this book into three sections: Past, Present and Future. Not on a whim, but as a map of my soul. A triple echo of my searches, my losses, my certainties, and my doubts.

If one thing unites these stories, it is the rope.

The symbolic rope that a character throws into a prison. Where truth is punished.

The invisible rope that pulls the reader with every page in a Morse code so interesting it could have many possible translations. Both of us, you and I, at either end. Strangers, but connected by a rope. The rope between the one who writes while sleeping and the one who reads while awake.

I don't rule out hunting dreams again. Who knows? Maybe a second collection will come. Or a complete work for each section. Or even one for each country. The tales are already circling. I hear them on my pillow and in the other spaces I've already confessed to. And I, who always have a place to write things down, prepare to receive them.

Thank you for reading.

Thank you for being on the other end of the rope. And for making it dance.

ACKNOWLEDGMENTS

First and foremost, I thank God for the gift of life and for the privilege of having lived it in three countries so rich in history and culture, which have been the canvas for many of these pages.

My infinite gratitude to my family, who are my foundation. Your unwavering belief in me has been my greatest inspiration, and so many of these stories were born from our shared experiences.

To my friends in so many parts of the world, those fellow travelers on this journey who, with true charity, show me my own blind spots and help me understand the footprints I leave behind. Thank you for the constructive criticism and the unwavering support.

My special thanks to Ninoshka Kniznik for being an early reader of this manuscript and for their valuable feedback.

And finally, to you, the reader. Whether you are family, a friend, a close acquaintance, or a complete stranger who has decided to delve into these stories, I thank you. Thank you for your trust, for your time, and for supporting this work. I hope that on this journey, you find something that resonates with you.

ABOUT THE AUTHOR

Rey Maya

 A poet, novelist, and storyteller whose life has unfolded in precise twenty-one-year cycles. His first was spent in Cuba, where his literary vocation was sparked by early acclaim for his poems and short stories. He then spent twenty-one years in Mexico, a formative period where he earned a degree in Educational Sciences while also studying Philosophy and Theology.

Now based in the United States, he balances his literary work with digital content creation.

He is the author of the novel Calambio and his debut short story collection, Beasts' Legacy: Past, Present and Future. He is currently at work on several new literary projects.